FIGHT 4 US
KEEPER

FIGHT 4 US
KEEPER

Copyright © 2018 by Brian Grenda

Printed in the United States of America

First Printing, 2018

FIGHT 4 US
KEEPER

CHAPTER 1
DON'T FEED THE ANIMALS

Armstrong aims his gun at the approaching lion and lioness as he stands next to Brimley and Roberts in the outdoor lion exhibit at the Tampa Zoo.

Armstrong shouts, "We need a way out of here TJ!"

Brimley and Roberts, who are standing slightly behind Armstrong, aim their rifles at the lion and lioness.

ROAR!

The male lion lets out a huge roar as he walks closer to Armstrong.

TJ sees a closed silver metal entrance door inside the lion exhibit.

TJ shouts, "Help! Please open the door! We don't want to have to kill these animals!"

Armstrong shouts, "Who are you yelling at? No one is here to help! We need to kill these animals!"

Brimley shouts, "Fuck this! I ain't dying for these people and this way!"

Brimley takes aims at the lions' head and puts his finger on the trigger.

Roberts follows suit and aims his rifle at the lioness' head.

A loud whistle goes off.

The lion, lioness, and everyone look up at the stone wall outside of the lion exhibit where the whistle came from.

A woman jumps up onto the stone border wall of the outdoor lion exhibit.

The woman whistles again.

The woman shouts, "Down Taraji! Down Zeus!"

The lion and lioness sit down in the grass but are still staring at Armstrong, Brimley, and Roberts.

"Put your guns down! Do not hurt my animals!" shouts the woman as she looks at Armstrong and TJ.

Armstrong, Brimley, and Roberts look at each other but keep their guns aimed on the lion and lioness.

TJ shouts, "Yes ma'am! Do what she says everyone!"

TJ goes to put his gun on the ground but sees that Armstrong now has his gun pointed at the woman, while Brimley and Roberts have their guns aimed at the lion and lioness still.

TJ holds his gun at his side and shouts, "Armstrong! Do what she says! Stand down!"

Armstrong shouts, "I can't do that TJ! I'm not putting my life and my men's lives in some woman's hands."

The woman shouts, "Sir with the gun pointed at me! I would listen to your friend there and lower your weapons! You have no place to go!"

Just as the woman finishes her statement, ten people come around the woman with guns and other weapons pointed at TJ, Armstrong, Bo, Brimley, Janet, and Roberts.

"One command and my animals will rip you apart. Do you want to live or die?" asks the woman.

Bo looks up at the woman and group of people standing around the woman on the stone border wall of the lion exhibit and shouts, "Barrett? Darby? Nicky?"

A man walks closer to the woman talking and shouts, "Bo! Is that you? What are you doing down there?"

Bo replies, "Looking for you. I came looking for you, Darby, and Nicky."

Janet shouts, "I hate to break up the family reunion, but can we get the fuck out here please! I don't like how your lion is staring at me!"

Zeus licks his lips as he stares at Janet.

Barrett shouts, "I'll be right down and get you out of there!"

Bo shouts, "Hey Darby! Hey Nicky!"

Darby says, "Hey Bo. Barrett will get you right out of there. I'll keep Zeus, Taraji, and Keanu from attacking."

Nicky shouts, "Where have you been Bo? I was worried sick about you!"

Armstrong shouts, "Enough with this bullshit! Get us out of here or I'll kill both of your animals."

Suddenly, a small lion cub runs over to the lioness Taraji.

Janet sees the cub and instantly worries about the safety of the animals.

Janet points her handgun at Armstrong and says, "Drop your damn gun. Don't be a moron. She clearly has command of these animals. They will get us out of here. Don't do anything stupid."

Brimley points his gun at Janet.

TJ points his gun at Brimley.

Bo steps back out of the way of Janet and TJ.

Armstrong looks at TJ and says, "You better control your girl TJ. She's gonna get us all killed."

TJ replies, "She is fine. You are the one not listening Armstrong."

Barrett opens the silver metal door inside the lion exhibit.

Barrett shouts, "Come on guys!"

Bo sees Barrett and walks through the animal entrance doorway, followed by Janet and TJ.

Armstrong, Brimley, and Roberts slowly walk towards the doorway Bo, Janet, and TJ went through.

Darby shouts, "Close the door Barrett!"

Barrett asks, "You sure Darby?"

Armstrong stops walking and looks up at Darby.

Darby shouts, "Close the door Barrett!"

Barrett closes the silver metal door.

Brimley shouts, "What do we do Armstrong?"

Armstrong shouts, "Keep your guns on the animals! Kill the cub first if we need too!"

Darby takes out her handgun and shoots the ground in front of Armstrong.

BANG!

Zeus lets out a big roar.

ROAR!

Darby shouts, "Zeus! Taraji! Keanu! Home!"

Zeus, Taraji, and their cub Keanu run back to their covered area at the opposite end of the lion exhibit away from Armstrong, Brimley, and Roberts.

As Keanu is running behind his mother Taraji, Armstrong takes aim at the cub.

Armstrong shouts, "You want to play games! I can play games too!"

Armstrong puts his finger on his rifle trigger and adjusts his aim onto Keanu's head.

Armstrong takes a deep breath.

Three gunshots go off.

BANG!

BANG!

BANG!

Keanu makes it safely around the tree where Zeus and Taraji are sitting.

"What the fuck are you doing?" shouts TJ with his handgun pointed at Armstrong.

Armstrong, Brimley, and Roberts look at TJ in disbelieve.

TJ and Janet shot the rifles out of the hands of Armstrong, Brimley, and Roberts.

TJ, Barrett, Bo, and Janet walk back into the lion exhibit through the animal entrance and over to Armstrong.

TJ shouts, "Why are you here Armstrong?"

Armstrong replies, "Your father gave us orders to join you on this trip."

Janet replies, "Obviously, but what are your orders? You don't know Bo, TJ, or myself, so you aren't here to save anyone. You are here to gain intel and report back?"

Armstrong looks at Brimley and Roberts and says, "We have our orders, but they are classified."

"Keep your guns pointed at them!" shouts TJ.

TJ sees the rifles of Armstrong, Brimley, and Roberts.

TJ walks to the dirt in front of Armstrong, Brimley, and Roberts.

Armstrong asks, "What are you doing TJ?"

TJ picks up the first two rifles and says, "I'm taking your weapons."

TJ goes to reach for the third rifle in front of Roberts.

Roberts watches TJ reach for the rifle and gets mad.

TJ grabs the rifle from the ground.

As TJ is standing up after grabbing Roberts' rifle, Roberts kicks TJ in the stomach.

TJ falls backwards onto the ground.

TJ drops the rifles as he lands on his back.

Roberts shouts, "No one takes my rifle!"

Roberts jumps on top of TJ and starts punching him in the face.

Janet points her gun at Roberts and shouts, "Roberts! Stop it! Get off him!"

Armstrong shouts, "Let them fight!"

Roberts rains down punches on TJ's face.

TJ defends himself but is getting bloodier in his face with each punch by Roberts.

Janet fires a shot in the air.

Roberts stops punching TJ and looks at Janet.

TJ grabs Roberts' left forearm, brings both of his legs around Roberts' left arm, shoulder, and neck.

Roberts grimaces in pain.

TJ looks at Roberts' face as he pulls down on Roberts' left arm with all his body weight.

SNAP!

TJ breaks Roberts' left arm.

Roberts screams in pain.

AHH!

TJ releases Roberts' left arm, stands up from the ground, and spits some blood from his mouth.

TJ shouts, "Tie them up! Restrain Armstrong and Brimley!"

Janet asks, "With what?"

Barrett says, "We have to have something in here we can use."

Barrett goes back through the lion exhibit animal entrance.

Roberts shouts, "You broke my freaking arm!"

TJ shouts, "You deserved it! You had no right to attack me!"

Armstrong looks at TJ and shouts, "I hope you know what you are doing!"

Barrett runs back out to Janet and asks, "I have these zip ties. Will they work?"

Janet says, "Yeah. They will work perfectly."

Bo and Janet zip tie Brimley and Armstrong's hands behind their back.

TJ walks over to Roberts and says, "I'm going to zip tie your hands in front of you. Don't fight it."

Roberts shouts, "Fuck you!"

TJ says, "Fair enough."

TJ smacks Roberts in the head with his handgun and knocks him out.

Roberts falls into the dirt.

A cloud of dust flies into the air as Roberts faceplants into the dirt.

TJ puts Roberts hands together and zip ties them together behind Roberts back.

Janet asks, "You okay TJ?"

TJ looks at Janet and says, "Yeah. I'm okay. My face is just swollen and bruised. Let's get them inside now."

Janet, Barrett, and Bo escort Armstrong and Brimley into the indoor lion cage room of the lion exhibit.

TJ drags Roberts into the indoor cage section and Barrett closes the silver door.

Armstrong and Brimley are positioned next to a wall, as Janet, Bo, Barrett, and TJ talk.

Bo hugs Barrett and says, "I'm so glad you are okay. I was worried sick about you."

Janet looks at TJ and asks, "What do we do with the three amigos over there?"

TJ looks at a sign, laughs, and says, "We can always feed them to the lions."

Bo introduces Barrett to Janet and TJ.

Armstrong looks at Brimley and nods his head.

Janet sees the interaction between Armstrong and Brimley and walks over to them.

"What's the plan fellas? I know you are trying to figure a way out of this," says Janet.

Armstrong says, "We will play nice now. We don't want to be fed to the animals."

Janet says, "I don't trust you. You Delta Force guys are nuts."

Janet takes Armstrong and Brimley's weapons that they have on them. Janet takes two knives, two grenades, and their two handguns from Armstrong and Brimley.

TJ says, "Good idea Janet."

TJ takes the weapons Roberts has on him as he is passed out on the concrete floor.

Darby, Nicky, and several other women enter the lion exhibit indoor cage area and walk over to Bo, TJ, Barrett, and Janet.

Nicky hugs Bo and gives him a big kiss.

Bo introduces TJ and Janet to his girlfriend Nicky and Barrett's fiancé Darby.

A woman comes over to Darby and says, "I don't trust those three men right there. I don't want them around Zeus, Taraji, and Keanu."

Darby looks at Armstrong and Brimley and says, "I don't trust them either Aisha. They will not be around the lions unless we are feeding them to Zeus."

11

Aisha smiles, looks at Darby, and says, "It is almost feeding time for big Zeus."

TJ and Darby make eye contact.

TJ says, "Darby, I just want to apologize for our landing in the lion exhibit. Our helicopter was taking gunfire and we had to decide on what to do. We meant no harm with this trip."

Bo says, "Darby, TJ and Janet are good people. They made this trip happen on blind faith of me finding Barrett and Nicky. You can trust TJ and Janet."

Darby looks at TJ and Janet and says with her Australian accent, "You showed me that I can trust you. You and Janet saved my lions. I am grateful for that, but I don't trust your three fellow soldiers."

A woman comes in the room and gives TJ a bag of ice to put on his bruised-up face.

TJ thanks the woman and applies the ice bag to the left side of his face, which is badly swollen, bruised, and bloody.

Darby asks, "Is your face okay TJ?"

TJ touches his face and says, "I don't think anything is broken. It's just swollen. I will be okay."

Armstrong shouts, "I hate to break up the party here, but you are going to let us go right?"

Roberts wakes up and lets out a big moan as he lays on the concrete floor.

Darby says, "We can have our doctor take a look at your man's arm."

Armstrong says, "Yeah. That's the least you could do. Patch up Roberts before you kick us out."

Darby walks over to Armstrong and shouts, "Excuse me? Least we can do? You came here to our home and started this! You are lucky we don't feed you to our animals!"

Armstrong smirks and says, "You ain't going to do nothing. You are all talk and trying to scare us."

Barrett walks over to Armstrong now.

Barrett is a large man. He stands 6 feet 4 inches tall and weighs 265 pounds.

Barrett looks at Armstrong and says, "Now mister. That's not nice picking on the little 5-foot 6 lady who weighs 135 pounds. I think you should apologize for the rude remarks you made and the previous attempts to kill her animals."

Armstrong laughs and replies, "Sure thing Barrett. What kind of a name is that anyway?"

Barrett replies, "I can see you are the smart ass of the group."

Barrett takes out a large knife from a holster behind his back.

Bo walks over to Barrett and says, "Brother, calm down. Don't do anything crazy with grandpa's knife."

Roberts tries to stand up but can't.

"Can someone help me get off the ground? It smells like shit over here!" shouts Roberts.

TJ walks over to Roberts and helps him stand up.

Darby opens an empty lion holding cage.

"Let's put them in here for now. They will be safe in here and they won't be able to get out unless we let them out," says Darby as she holds open the steel cage door.

TJ puts Roberts in the cage.

Bo and Barrett escort Armstrong and Brimley into the same cage as Roberts.

Darby closes and locks the steel cage door.

TJ looks at Armstrong and asks, "Do you want to tell me why you are here with us? What are your orders?"

Armstrong just stares at TJ from inside the cage.

"Okay. Don't talk now when it's easy. Just remember where you are and what animals are waiting outside to eat," says TJ.

Darby, Nicky, Aisha, and the rest of Darby's group take TJ, Bo, Barrett, and Janet out of the indoor lion exhibit cage area and out to the main complex of the zoo.

TJ walks by a sign and over to Janet.

The sign reads, "DON'T FEED THE ANIMALS."

Bo walks with Nicky and Barrett.

"How did you get into this place Barrett?" asks Bo.

Barrett replies, "I drove my truck here when they were building the walls. The walls were pretty much done except for a small section. I shouted for Darby, and Nicky found me. Nicky told me how to get in, but I had to leave my truck outside."

Nicky says, "We have ways in and out of the zoo. The walls are very secure, but we do have some hidden ways to get in and out."

Bo says, "I'd say your walls are very secure. I didn't know how to get in. None of us did."

The group walks towards a main center section of the large zoo.

Barrett looks at TJ and asks, "You took some gunfire on the way here?"

TJ replies, "Yeah. One second it was all clear, and then suddenly our helicopter took on some heavy gunfire. I didn't see who was shooting at us, but our pilot made the quick decision to get away from the gunfire."

Barrett looks at Nicky and says, "I'm sure it was Isiah's people."

Janet asks, "Isiah? Is he good or bad?"

Nicky replies, "He's good. He's on our side. He and his people watch over this place for us. They protect the wall and borders."

Barrett says, "Isiah and his group are good people. A little strange, but they protect the zoo and people inside the wall. Darby and her people were attacked in here before the walls went up. People even tried to attack us when the walls were finished."

TJ walks by an empty rhino exhibit and then an empty giraffe exhibit.

"What happened to the rhinos and giraffes?" asks TJ.

Darby shouts, "Hunters, people, and zombies killed them! They killed some of our other animals also! Before the walls went up! Some animals escaped and could be anywhere in the Tampa Bay area now! Our lions, baby elephant, gorilla, chimpanzee and her babies, and two orangutans are still alive though!"

Janet says, "I'm sorry to hear about you being attacked."

Darby stops walking in the center of a zoo walkway and says, "Me too. We are secure in here for now. As long as I'm the keeper of this zoo, I will protect this place."

Darby is the leader of this group. She is Barrett's fiancé and moved to Tampa Bay by way of Australia several years ago.

Several people walk over to Darby and Aisha.

TJ, Barrett, Janet, and Bo look at Darby.

Barrett whispers to Bo, "I call Darby and her group, the Pride. They are mostly women here. Darby is the head lioness to her group of lionesses'."

Janet overhears Barrett talking to Bo and whispers, "Better watch out. In the wild, the lioness does the hunting and is pretty badass. This group of women doesn't look to be messing around."

Darby looks at TJ, Janet, and Bo and says, "Welcome TJ, Janet, and Barrett's brother Bo to our home. I think we can trust you. Bo, Janet, and TJ were looking for Barrett. Do not hold anything against Bo, Janet, or TJ. They mean no harm and I believe them."

Darby's group stares at TJ, Janet, and Bo.

TJ feels somewhat uncomfortable with the continuous stares that Darby's group is giving him.

TJ says, "Thank you, Darby and everyone. Janet, Bo, and I mean no harm to you, your group, or your home. I apologize for just dropping in on you like we did, but your border wall is making it very hard for anyone to get in."

Darby says, "That's the point."

A woman in a white medical coat walks over to Darby.

Darby looks at the woman and says, "Dr. Adler. We have a man with a potentially broken arm in the lion cages. I want you to check him out, but do not go alone. He and his men are dangerous. You are to examine him with a large group for safety."

Dr. Adler replies, "Yes ma'am. I will go with a group to check him out."

Nicky walks over to Bo and says, "Let me show you guys around. This place is pretty incredible."

Barrett walks over to Darby.

Nicky takes Bo, TJ, and Janet around the zoo and the rest of the property inside the wall.

CHAPTER 2
THE PRIDE

"You have a supermarket and shopping center in here?" shouts Janet.

Nicky says, "Yeah. The border wall just doesn't stop around the zoo. It goes around several streets and buildings near downtown Tampa. Darby was smart when she built the borders around the zoo, shopping center, and supermarket."

Bo, Barrett, Darby, Nicky, TJ, and Janet are standing in the street as they look at the supermarket inside the borders of the wall.

The supermarket is a couple streets away from the zoo entrance.

Darby says, "We are secure in here. We have most of the things needed to survive. We need to get supplies from outside our borders from time to time though. Our animals require a lot of food and water."

"How do you feed two lions and a cub?" asks Bo.

Barrett says, "With people."

Bo laughs and asks, "You serious?"

Darby says, "We don't feed them people, but we found out early on that the animals can eat the zombies and not get sick. We try not to feed our lions zombie meat all the time, but we do from time to time. We try to give them fresh turned zombies if possible."

Nicky says, "It's hard finding food for all our

animals. We have a baby elephant, gorilla, a chimpanzee with two babies, goats, two orangutans, and a tortoise."

Janet asks, "How do you power the supermarket?"

Darby replies, "We don't have power going to it. We don't have electricity in here yet. We just got a bunch of solar panels but haven't connected them yet."

Dr. Adler walks over to Darby and asks, "Can I go check on the soldier's now?"

TJ, Janet, and Bo look at Darby.

Darby says, "Yeah. Let's go check him out."

TJ says, "We are going with you. We need to get information out of them."

Dr. Adler walks towards the lion exhibit employee entrance door.

TJ walks with Dr. Adler and says, "Doc. I want to interrogate these men. I want to use Roberts injury to get information out of them."

"You want to torture him?" asks Dr. Adler.

Janet says, "Basically, but these guys are tough. It might be the only way to get information out of them."

Dr. Adler says, "Let me check him out first before you torture him."

Dr. Adler, TJ, Janet, Bo, and Barrett enter the employee entrance to the indoor lion cage area.

Dr. Adler walks over to the cage that is holding Armstrong, Roberts, and Brimley.

Dr. Adler goes to open the cage but is stopped by TJ.

"Wait doc, I have to make sure they won't use you as a hostage first," says TJ.

TJ looks at Armstrong, Brimley, and Roberts inside the lion cage and shouts, "Turn around! Show me your hands!"

Armstrong stands up from the ground with his hands behind his back and starts laughing.

"What? You don't trust us TJ?" asks Armstrong.

TJ replies, "Nope."

Janet picks up a tennis ball from a nearby table, walks over to the lion cage, and throws the tennis ball at Armstrong's face.

The tennis ball comes flying at Armstrong's face.

Armstrong catches the ball with his right hand.

"I knew we couldn't trust them," says Janet.

Armstrong tosses the tennis ball up in the air and catches it with his untied right hand.

Brimley and Roberts bring their arms from behind their back and show them to TJ.

Armstrong, Brimley, and Roberts broke free from the zip ties.

"See doc. They might have used you to get free. Held you hostage. These men are very capable and will do anything to get what they want," says TJ.

"That's very true TJ," says Armstrong.

Dr. Adler says, "Roberts is it? Come here so I can check your arm."

Roberts walks towards Dr. Adler.

Dr. Adler says, "Let me see your arm."

Roberts leans towards Dr. Adler.

TJ grabs Roberts left arm and pulls Roberts into the cage bars.

Roberts screams in pain.

AHH!

Dr. Adler looks at TJ and says, "Let him go TJ."

TJ stares at Roberts and says, "I will doc. Just need to get some information first. Why are you here Roberts?"

Roberts shouts, "Fuck you!"

TJ pulls Roberts' left arm harder towards him and Roberts' face presses into the bars of the lion cage.

Armstrong shouts, "What do you want to know TJ? Stop torturing Roberts! He doesn't know anything! I do!"

TJ holds onto Roberts' left arm and shouts, "Why are you here? Why did my father send you with us?"

Armstrong shouts, "Let him go and I'll tell you!"

Janet shouts, "No way! You tell us first and TJ will let Roberts go!"

Armstrong tosses the tennis ball through the bars to Janet.

Armstrong looks at TJ and says, "We were sent here to help you. Get in and out of the zoo but also gather any intel we could about what is in here and who is in here. Several helicopters have been shot at when they fly over the zoo and parts of downtown Tampa. Your father wants to know who is shooting and why."

TJ lets go of Roberts' arm.

Roberts takes a deep breath and says, "Thanks a lot fucker."

TJ looks right at Armstrong and asks, "So, you are supposed to gain intel about this place and report back? Why? So, someone can attack it or take it over?"

Aisha looks at Darby with a worried look.

Darby walks over to TJ and looks at Armstrong.

"Who wants in here? Who will be attacking us?" asks Darby.

Armstrong smirks and says, "The U.S. government is coming to Tampa Bay. The military and government want to take over all viable areas. This place is definitely on their radar."

TJ looks at Janet.

Nicky looks at Bo.

Darby looks at Aisha and then Barrett.

"How much time do we have?" asks Darby to Armstrong.

Armstrong says, "You let us out of here, and I'll tell you."

Barrett shouts, "You ain't getting out of there unless we trust you!"

Roberts asks, "Can we get some water at least?"

Dr. Adler says, "That we can do."

Darby says, "We can't just let you out. You tried to kill my lions and you attacked TJ. We don't want any trouble from anyone. We want to be left alone. We aren't bothering anyone, but so many people are interested in what we have here. I know how the world works and how dangerous you three soldiers are."

Armstrong says, "Fair enough. Just remember though. The longer we stay here, more troops will be sent here to come find us. If we don't come back to MacDill alive, the military will send in tanks and tons of soldiers to destroy this place."

TJ looks at Darby and says, "He's bluffing. He's not that important. Don't worry about that. My father is the Captain at MacDill Air Force Base. I will protect this place and your Pride."

Armstrong laughs and shouts, "Captain Bailey isn't the one you have to worry about! The General is the one with the real power!"

A woman brings in three bottles of water.

TJ takes the bottles of water and takes the caps off all three bottles. He takes a big drink from each bottle of water and then places the bottles on the lion cage floor.

Armstrong runs towards the bottles of water and grabs the bottles of water.

Everyone jumps back from the cage.

Darby shouts, "Everyone out of here! I need to talk with these soldiers! TJ and Janet stay with me!"

Everyone exits the room except TJ, Janet, and Darby.

Armstrong shouts, "Your only chance of saving this place is to let myself and my men out of here and let me talk with Captain Bailey!"

Darby looks at Armstrong and says, "I want to let you out of here, but I'm not sure that I can. This place, my animals, and my people mean everything to me. If I let you go, how do I know you won't just come back here with an army?"

Armstrong looks at Brimley and Roberts.

TJ looks at Darby and says, "We can't let them go and not expect problems. If we let them go back to MacDill, they will be back here with a large group."

Armstrong says, "This place isn't that important to me. I wish you would believe that, but I'm not sure I can say anything to make this situation better."

Darby isn't sure what to do. She looks at Janet and TJ for help.

Janet says, "Let's get out of here and take a break from this situation. We need to talk privately away from these three."

TJ says, "Good idea. These three aren't going anywhere. We will be back."

TJ pulls the metal lion cage door and makes sure the cage is locked.

Darby places the lion cage key on a wooden table near the exit of the room.

Janet, Darby, and TJ exit the lion cage room.

TJ opens the employee lion exhibit exit door.

Janet, Darby, and then TJ exit the exhibit.

"What do we do with these three soldiers? We are not killers here. We just want to be left alone in here. We will protect this place, but I don't feel right just killing those men," says Darby.

Janet replies, "I understand Darby. I don't want to just kill them either, but we can't have them report back any information about this place."

Aisha runs over to Darby and says, "What if we blindfold them and took them out the back exit? We have their weapons. They won't see anything if we blindfold them, and they won't know anything besides that we have lions and we are living in the zoo."

Darby says, "I like the idea of having them not knowing anything about this place but also being kept alive."

TJ says, "We will figure something out. I will get back to my father and report our findings here. Janet and I will tell my father that this place is not worth the military's time and to leave it alone."

Darby says, "Thank you. I appreciate it. My animals and my people appreciate it."

"Do you have a bathroom around here?" asks TJ.

Darby says, "There is one over there on your left. Right after the bird sanctuary entrance."

TJ walks away from Darby and down the path towards the bird sanctuary.

Janet shouts, "Wait up TJ!"

Janet catches up to TJ, and they walk towards the bathrooms.

TJ says, "This place won't stand a chance if the military decides to attack it. The walls are great, but they won't hold up against tanks and rockets."

23

Janet stops at the entrance to the ladies' bathroom and says, "We can't let Armstrong, Brimley, and Roberts live. I'm sure you already knew that though."

TJ says, "Yeah, I knew that once Roberts attacked me. I didn't want to say it in front of Darby and the others though."

Janet says, "I gotta pee. We will figure something out though."

TJ and Janet go into separate bathrooms.

Bo looks at Barrett and asks, "Are you coming back home with me today?"

Barrett replies, "I will be back home, but I'm not leaving until the soldiers are gone. I won't feel comfortable until the soldier situation is dealt with."

Bo asks, "What do you suggest we do?"

Barrett says, "We need to handle it one way or another."

Bo checks his handguns and says, "I agree."

Nicky comes over to Bo and asks, "What's going on fellas? Can you help us connect the solar panels around the zoo and supermarket?"

Bo says, "Yeah, Barrett and I will help you connect the solar panels."

Nicky kisses Bo and says, "Thanks baby."

Darby comes over to Barrett.

Darby sees the look in Barrett's eyes.

"What's up honey bear?" asks Darby.

Barrett says, "I don't feel comfortable with these soldiers and having them locked up here. They are dangerous and keeping them alive is dangerous for you and your Pride."

Darby says, "You really like calling us the Pride. I like that name, and I appreciate the concern. I can't kill them though. I won't be able to live with myself if I was responsible for killing another living person."

Bo says, "We would never ask you to do that, but we were thinking we could take care of them for you and your Pride."

Barrett kisses Darby and says, "Let us take care of them. You have enough to worry about around here."

Before Darby can reply, Bo and Barrett walk away from Darby.

Darby isn't sure what to do.

Darby watches Bo and Barrett enter the lion exhibit employee entrance.

A member of the Pride comes over to Darby and says, "We have a little situation with Louie and the chimps."

Darby says, "I'll be right there."

The woman, Nicky, and the rest of the Pride make their way over to the primate section of the zoo.

Darby looks at the lion exhibit employee entrance door and isn't sure if she should stop Bo and Barrett.

Janet and TJ walk over to Darby.

"What's going on? Why did your group go running away from here?" asks Janet.

Darby says, "We have a situation with our gorilla and our chimps."

TJ asks, "Where is Bo and Barrett?"

Darby looks back at the lion exhibit employee door.

TJ asks, "Are they in there with the soldiers?"

Darby starts to cry and says, "Yes. Yes, they are."

TJ runs towards the lion exhibit employee door.

BANG!

A gunshot is heard as TJ stops at the lion exhibit employee entrance door.

TJ opens the door and runs into the indoor lion cage area.

BANG!

Another gunshot goes off.

Janet runs to the outdoor lion exhibit.

Janet sees the animal entrance to the indoor lion cage area is open.

Zeus is walking towards the opening that leads into the indoor cage area.

BANG!

Another gunshot goes off from inside the lion cages.

Janet shouts, "Darby! We have a problem here!"

Darby runs over to Janet and sees that Zeus is walking towards the indoor lion cage area.

ROAR!

Zeus roars as he peeks his head through the animal entrance into the indoor cage area.

A loud scream is heard as Zeus enters the indoor lion cage area.

AHHHH!

BANG!

Another gunshot goes off inside the lion cages.

Darby screams in fear.

AHH!

Janet and Darby run towards the lion indoor exhibit employee entrance door.

Before Darby and Janet make it to the door, TJ comes running out of the door.

TJ holds open the door, and Bo exits followed by Barrett.

Barrett is bleeding from his left shoulder.

"What happened?" asks Darby.

"I opened the lion cage. Brimley reached for my gun

after I shot Roberts in the head. Brimley got my gun. He got a shot off, but he only got me on the outside of my left shoulder. Bo killed Brimley," says Barrett.

Bo says, "They are all dead now. TJ killed Armstrong."

TJ asks, "What was the plan fellas? Kill them, so we didn't have to deal with them anymore?"

Barrett says, "I couldn't leave them alive. I'm looking after this place. Armstrong was a threat. I had to neutralize the threat."

Darby asks, "Is Zeus okay?"

Before anyone can answer, Darby runs to the lion exhibit stone border wall and blows her lion whistle.

Taraji and Keanu come running towards the sound of the whistle.

Zeus is nowhere to be found.

Darby blows her whistle again.

Taraji and Keanu roar at Darby.

ROAR!

A loud roar is heard from inside the lion cages.

Suddenly, Zeus comes walking out from the indoor lion cage room animal entrance.

Zeus is licking his lips with his tongue.

Zeus' mouth and cheeks are bright red, and blood is dripping from his mouth as he is walking towards his lioness Taraji and cub Keanu.

Darby starts to cry as she sees Zeus and his bloody mouth.

Janet says, "Well, that looks to be settled. You okay TJ?"

TJ says, "Yeah. I'm okay. They are all dead now. Zeus was biting into Roberts when we left the room."

Darby shouts, "Zeus! Taraji! Keanu! Home!"

Taraji, Zeus, and Keanu run to the shaded area in the outdoor lion exhibit and sit under a group of trees.

Darby walks over to Barrett and asks, "Are you okay? Is the bullet in your arm?"

Barrett lifts up his left arm shirt sleeve and Darby examines his gunshot wound.

Darby says, "Just looks like a flesh wound. We'll have Dr. Adler stitch you up."

Janet looks at TJ and says, "Let's check out the lion cages and the remains of the three amigos."

TJ, Bo, and Janet go back into the lion exhibit cage room.

"Holy crap!" shouts Janet as she looks at the bodies of Armstrong, Brimley, and Roberts.

There is a ton of blood on the floor, walls, and steel cage bars. The bodies of Armstrong, Brimley, and Roberts were ripped apart by Zeus.

"Zeus must have bit into each of them," says TJ.

The bodies of Brimley, Roberts, and Armstrong are cut, bloody, and have big bite marks in them.

"What should we do with the bodies?" asks Janet.

Bo walks over to a pair of rubber boots and takes off his cowboy boots.

TJ walks over to Bo and starts taking off his military boots.

Bo and TJ put on a pair of rubber boots and gloves.

Bo walks into the lion cage and starts removing articles of clothing and gear from Roberts' dead body.

Bo is taking off everything from Roberts' body that he doesn't want the lions to eat.

TJ checks out Brimley's body and removes Brimley's boots and vest.

Bo drags Roberts' chewed up body towards the

animal entrance of the outdoor lion exhibit.

TJ grabs Brimley's legs and drags his bloody body towards the animal entrance of the lion exhibit.

TJ drops Brimley's dead body next to Roberts' dead body.

Bo pushes Roberts' body out into the dirt of the lion exhibit and then pushes Brimley's body through the animal entrance.

TJ walks back into the lion cage and grabs Armstrong's mauled body.

Armstrong has a huge gash and several claw marks on his face and chest.

TJ removes Armstrong's boots and then drags Armstrong's dead body along the bloody floor and towards the lion outdoor exhibit animal entrance.

Blood is pouring out of Armstrong's chest and head as TJ drags his lifeless body.

TJ and Bo remove Armstrong's vest and then push Armstrong's body through the animal entrance and onto the dirt.

Bo hears the lions running towards the bodies and quickly closes the silver metal door.

Zeus, Taraji, and Keanu start attacking and eating the bodies of Armstrong, Brimley, and Roberts.

Janet says, "Good job guys. Those three were assholes anyway."

Bo says, "Barrett and I couldn't risk having them attack this place. Darby, Nicky, and the Pride don't need the government coming down on them."

TJ looks at Bo and says, "I will do my best to keep this place safe."

Bo says, "I hope so."

CHAPTER 3
WHAT DID YOU GET ME?

I open my SUV trunk and look at what I got from World of Trade.

As I stand in my driveway, I hear Bobby G's front door open.

Bobby G walks out his front door with Odin.

Phil looks at Bobby G and asks, "Hey Bob? Why do you have Odin with you?"

Bobby G replies, "TJ left him with me, until you guys came back. He wanted you or Shaun to watch Odin while he is away on his trip to the zoo."

I overhear Bobby G talking with Phil and walk over to Phil, Bobby G, and Odin.

Odin looks up at me as he sits down on Bobby G's driveway.

"How long ago did TJ leave?"

Bobby G replies, "Probably three hours or so ago. Bo, Janet, and TJ left Odin here and then went to MacDill."

My house front door opens.

Lauren walks outside and sees that I made it back home. She walks to my SUV trunk and starts looking at what is in my SUV trunk.

I see Lauren looking in my World of Trade boxes and I walk over to my SUV.

"Excuse me lady. What are you looking for?"

Lauren jokes, "What did you get me?"

I cover the box of stuff I got from World of Trade and say, "It's a surprise. I will show you later."

Lauren laughs and says, "Great. I'll be back later. I'm going over to Nicole's to check on the babies."

Lauren walks over to Matt's house and goes inside.

I grab a box of stuff I got from World of Trade and walk over to Bobby G.

Bobby G looks at me and asks, "What did you get? How was World of Trade?"

Phil says, "It was pretty good. They have tons of stuff there. We have to go back soon. I saw a couple more things I want to get for my SUV and some other goodies."

I hand Bobby G the box and say, "Here ya go Bob. I got some good stuff for ya."

Bobby G puts the box on top of Phil's SUV hood and starts looking inside the box. Bobby G is like a kid on Christmas morning. He's excited to see all the things I got him.

Bobby G pulls out a brand-new military style hat and puts it on his head.

"Awesome. Thank you. I had a hat just like this back home. I forgot to bring it though. It was that military style hat we got in Orlando at my first zombie convention," says Bobby G.

"I remember that hat. I still have mine from that day we went to our first zombie convention in Orlando."

It's funny how a simple item can make you remember a day or experience. I can clearly remember that whole day with my dad. It was our first zombie convention and it was great. That was many years ago, but it was a memorable experience, and that hat makes me remember it.

I look at my dad wearing the hat and joke, "That hat will cover up that chrome dome of yours."

Bobby G, Phil, and I laugh.

Bobby G says, "Thank you for the gifts Ryan. Phil, can you or Shaun take Odin?"

Phil says, "I wouldn't mind taking Odin, but I think Shaun wants Odin. He misses not having a dog."

Bobby G replies, "Okay great. TJ left me some food for Odin in my house."

Phil says, "Shaun or I will come by later to get Odin and the food. You enjoy spending time with him for a little longer."

Bobby G says, "Okay great. I'll be inside my house if you need me for anything."

Odin and Bobby G walk back into Bobby G's house.

Matt and Shaun exit from Matt's house and walk over to my SUV.

"Why won't you show me what you got from World of Trade?" asks Shaun.

Matt replies, "Because it's personal man."

I look at Matt and Shaun as they are standing in my driveway.

Phil and I walk over to Shaun and Matt.

"Everything okay guys?"

"Yeah. Everything is fine. Shaun is just being nosy is all," says Matt.

Shaun replies, "I gave you one of those awesome survival kits I got. I was just curious what you got from our trip."

Matt looks at Phil.

I notice the look Matt gave Phil and become interested in what Matt is hiding.

"Everything okay Matt? You usually aren't the quiet

type when it comes to things. I remember you were all about that cashmere sweater that one Christmas."

Matt laughs and says, "That was my first Christmas with Kylie. We just started dating that summer."

Matt smiles and gets red in the face.

I see that Matt wants to say something but he's hesitating for some reason.

Matt looks down the street and around my SUV.

"I was just nervous to tell anyone the news. It's brand new information, and I didn't want to jinx anything," says Matt.

"What's up Matt?"

Matt looks at me and says, "Kylie is pregnant. She just found out a couple of days ago."

Shaun, Phil, and I cheer.

"That's great man. I'm excited for you guys."

"Congrats Matt. That's awesome," says Shaun as he shakes Matt's hand.

Matt replies, "I got a bunch of baby supplies and clothes at World of Trade. I know it's really early for that stuff, but I was excited when I saw the baby supplies and clothes."

I am very excited at the baby news but also very nervous for Matt and Kylie. The guys and I will do everything we can for Matt, Kylie, and the baby.

Babies and children are the future of the world. They always have been and always will be. The only thing that has changed is the type of world they will be inheriting.

"Man, you guys are going to need a bigger house. Four adults and three children living in that one house," says Shaun.

I look at Phil.

Matt sees me look at Phil.

"What's up Ryan?" asks Matt.

I look at Matt and say, "Nothing. I'm just happy for you and Kylie."

"Thanks, Ryan. We will be coming to you for advice and help. I'm sure. I wonder if there are any baby doctors alive anymore?" asks Matt.

"I hope so. I hope there are tons of medical professionals still alive and ready to help everyone. I can't be the only doctor left alive."

Shaun asks, "What's the next step Ryan? Any plans for the next couple of days?"

I take out the box of supplies I got for Lauren from my SUV trunk and look at Shaun.

"I have to meet Kat at the Big Club tomorrow around 10:30 but nothing other than that. Just have to see about TJ, the zoo, William, and Jacob."

Phil looks at Shaun and says, "Bobby G has Odin. TJ left Odin with Bobby G, but TJ wants myself or you to watch Odin until he comes back here."

Matt closes my SUV trunk, while I'm holding my box from World of Trade.

Shaun looks at Phil and says, "I'd love to take Odin for a little while. I miss having a dog."

I say goodbye to Matt, Phil, and Shaun.

The guys say goodbye and keep talking near Phil's SUV.

I walk into my house and place the box I was holding on the kitchen counter.

Milo runs to the open front door and looks out.

"Get back in here belly man!" I shout to Milo as he looks out the open front door.

I close my front door.

Milo runs into the living room.

I walk back into the kitchen and start taking out the contents of my box.

I organize the items that I got at World of Trade on my quartz kitchen countertop.

I make three piles of items.

One pile for me. One pile for Lauren, and one pile for both of us.

World of Trade had a lot of items, but I made sure to get some things that Lauren would like to have.

Callie walks into the kitchen and meows at me.

I look down at Callie as she sits next to the kitchen pantry.

"What do you want Callie girl?"

Callie looks up at me and meows again.

I walk over to the kitchen cabinet and get out the box of treats that Callie likes.

Callie walks over to her bowl that is next to the kitchen pantry.

My front door opens, and Lauren enters our house.

I fill Callie's bowl with several treats and Callie starts to eat them.

Lauren walks into the kitchen and says, "Look at all this great stuff you got. Oh man. You got a ton of chocolate. Thank you honey."

I walk over to Lauren and Lauren kisses me.

"You are welcome sweetie."

Lauren grabs a piece of dark chocolate and starts to unwrap the packaging.

"How was World of Trade? How was Jacob?" asks Lauren.

"It was pretty good. Jacob couldn't get us into level two, but we saw level one and got to shop a little bit."

Lauren replies, "I would like to go next time. If you think it's a good idea for me to go?"

"It's definitely crazy. People are everywhere. Vendors are tough. I even saw someone get killed for taking a piece of fruit. You can go if you think you can handle being around some crazy people and vendors."

Lauren looks at her pile of goods on the kitchen countertop and says, "I don't know if I need to go. I can give you a list of things again. You did a good job with this trip."

I wash my hands in the kitchen sink and Lauren starts putting away the goods I got from World of Trade.

Lauren picks up the bottle of champagne I got and says, "Very nice. Two bottles. Man, you really went all out for us."

I walk by Lauren, smack her butt, and say, "Anything for you my love."

I walk over to my man cave door, unlock the door, and walk into my man cave.

I turn on the lights and sit down in my recliner chair.

My man cave has been my room to relax, play video games, meditate, and just have some alone time.

As I sit in my recliner, I see a wall calendar on the wall next to a bookshelf.

I walk over to the calendar and see that it's not on the right month. The month on the calendar is May, which was the month of our guys trip to Tennessee.

Several months have gone by since our guys trip which was in the middle of May.

I flip the calendar month pages to August and then to September.

I really am not sure whether it's the end of August or early September. Time flies in a zombie apocalypse.

Lauren knocks on the man cave door, takes a step in the room, and asks, "You okay in here Ry?"

Lauren walks into the man cave and sees me looking at my golf clubs.

I pick up my nine-iron golf club and say, "I'm okay sweetie. Do you know what day it is?"

Lauren looks at the calendar and says, "The 30th of August. I think. I really don't know to be honest."

"I wonder when the outbreak started? How it started? Why it started?" I ask Lauren as I put my golf club back into my golf bag.

Lauren says, "I don't know. You went on your golf trip with the guys in the middle of May. I remember hearing weird stories on the news about some virus, people getting sick, people eating other people's faces, some project going on at the International Mall, the football stadium conversion, and old baseball stadium being turned into some camp or something."

"Yeah. I remember some of those stories. Especially the ones about the football stadium and old baseball stadium. I still can't believe the Tampa Bay baseball team left the area."

I walk out of my man cave with Lauren.

Milo is waiting outside of the man cave doorway.

Lauren picks up Milo.

"Milo is such a big boy. He's probably the only one who has gained weight since the zombie apocalypse started," jokes Lauren.

I close my man cave door.

Lauren walks into the living room and sets Milo down.

Milo goes to drink some water from his water bowl.

I walk into the living room and sit next to Lauren on

37

our big sectional sofa.

Lauren looks at the television and says, "I kind of wish we knew what was going on around the world and around here. Especially in Tampa, St. Petersburg. Clearwater, and south Florida."

I grab Lauren's hand and say, "I have totally forgotten about your parents. I wonder how they are doing in Boca Raton."

Lauren says, "I didn't want to bring up my parents with all the craziness going on around here. I'm not sure how they are doing."

"When was the last communication with them?"

"I talked to my mom months ago, when the phones worked. She was going with my father to my aunt and uncle's house. They were thinking about going to The Villages near Ocala, but I'm not sure if they ever made it there or if they are even alive," says Lauren.

"If you want to make a trip down to Boca, I will go with you. We will just have to make sure we have enough gas to make it down and back."

Lauren says, "I would like that. I have been worrying about them since the craziness started around here."

"I wouldn't mind getting away from here for a little bit and checking on Fran and Keith. I can see your dad surviving and hoarding tons of food and water from the supermarket."

Lauren laughs and says, "Yeah, but he has that bad shoulder and my mom can't hear anything. They weren't in the best shape before the zombies arrived."

"Well, you let me know when you want to go. I just have to meet someone at the Big Club tomorrow. I met this woman at the World of Trade and setup a meeting at the

Big Club with her."

"Hot date tomorrow with some woman?" jokes Lauren.

I laugh and reply, "No. She was someone I helped at World of Trade and she's a nurse. Her name is Kat. I felt a need to help her, and I'm glad I did. She was going to attack a vendor over some household supplies. They would have killed her if she attacked that vendor."

"I'm glad you helped her sweetie. I was only kidding about the hot date. Unless we are having one? We do have two bottles of champagne now," says Lauren.

"I like that idea sweetie. I think we are overdue for a nice date. We can have a nice dinner and watch a movie."

"Dinner and a movie. I like that," says Lauren.

"I'm going to the Big Club around 9 tomorrow morning. I haven't been there for a while and I wouldn't mind doing an inventory check of our supplies also. Do you want to come with me?"

Lauren says, "Yeah. I would like to go with you. The last time I was there was for the meeting with Jacob. It was pretty stressful. I hope this trip is much different."

"I'm sure it will be better this time and far less stressful."

Lauren and I enjoy the day and night together.

It's the next morning.

I awake from my bed and hear the rain hitting the roof as I sit at the edge of my bed.

Lauren is asleep still.

I check my watch and see that it says 7:44AM.

I walk over to Lauren who sleeps on the left side of our King-sized bed and kiss her forehead.

Lauren wakes up and asks, "Hey, everything okay?"

"Yeah. It's 7:45. I want to leave for the Big Club in

about an hour. What do you want for breakfast?"

Lauren says, "I'm going to make some oatmeal. I'll be up in a couple minutes."

I walk into the kitchen and take out two bowls and two packets of apple cinnamon oatmeal.

I look out the kitchen window and see that it's raining. It's raining hard this morning, my lawn and the crops in the backyard could use the rain. Our rain barrels were getting low as well. Water goes pretty fast around the neighborhood and it's a welcomed sight to see the rain barrels starting to fill up again.

Lauren walks into the kitchen and makes her oatmeal.

I set the table with our placemats.

Callie looks up at me as she stands next to her treat bowl.

"Morning Callie girl. I will fill your bowl up."

Callie meows at me as I walk into the kitchen.

Lauren fills up Milo's food bowl and replenishes the water bowls for Callie and Milo.

The microwave beeps, and Lauren takes out her bowl of oatmeal.

Lauren puts my bowl of oatmeal in the microwave now.

The kitchen smells like cinnamon.

I pour two glasses of orange juice and put them on the table.

Callie eats her treats from her bowl next to the kitchen pantry.

Milo eats his food from his bowl in the corner of the living room.

The microwave beeps, and Lauren takes out my bowl of oatmeal.

I grab the two bowls of oatmeal and place them on our dining room table placemats.

I sit down at the dining table and Lauren joins me.

"It's really raining outside there. Hopefully it will cool down a little now. It's been so hot this summer," says Lauren as she sits down in the chair next to me.

"I hope so. It's been pretty hot. August in Tampa, Florida is pretty hot. I can't wait for the cool down we should get in December."

Lauren and I enjoy a nice breakfast together.

As Lauren and I are eating breakfast this morning, I take a second to enjoy the moment.

I can't remember the last time Lauren and I had a nice relaxing breakfast together. It feels nice to just relax and have some time alone with Lauren.

Lauren and I finish breakfast and get ready for our trip to the Big Club.

"Do I need to bring anything?" asks Lauren.

I put on a red athletic shirt and say, "Bring your weapons like it's a normal run. Your bow, some bolts for your bow, and your handgun. We could run into some trouble on this trip and whenever we leave Citrus Oaks. Always be ready."

Lauren says, "Okay. I will be ready. Just wanted to make sure."

Lauren gears up for the trip and takes her weapons and gear to my SUV.

I finish getting dressed, put on my bulletproof vest, grab my handgun, an empty bag, and my katana.

The bulletproof vest still has the bullet in it from when Derrick shot me.

I glance down at the bullet, and I think back to that day in Orlando when Derrick shot me.

I say goodbye to Callie and Milo and exit through my front door.

Lauren is talking with Phil under our covered front porch.

I lock my front door and walk over to Phil and Lauren.

"What's up Phil?"

Phil asks, "Going to the Big Club today?"

"Yeah. What are you doing up so early? Couldn't sleep in your new house?"

Phil replies, "I slept pretty good actually. I like my new house. I'm just out for a run. I gotta stay in shape. I enjoy running and plan on running in the mornings now."

"I'll join ya. We can start a morning running routine. I miss running. I haven't had a good run since our trip to Tennessee."

Phil replies, "Sounds like a plan. I'll be by the Big Club later today. I haven't been there in a while."

"Sounds good Phil. I'll see ya later. Stay dry. I don't know how you are running in this rain."

"I like the rain. It cools me down. I'll see ya later," says Phil.

Phil runs out from my covered front porch and towards Buck's house.

Lauren and I run through the rain and get into my SUV.

I start up the engine and reverse out of my driveway.

I drive through the South entrance and towards the Big Club to meet with Kat.

CHAPTER 4
WHAT'S OUR AGREEMENT?

I pull up to the Big Club and it looks great.

I park my SUV near the front entrance of the Big Club.

There is a light rain sprinkle coming down onto the windshield of my SUV.

Lauren looks through the windows of my SUV and says, "The coast is clear, and the front entrance looks to be in good shape."

I grab the bag and my katana from the backseat.

Lauren takes her bow and bolts.

We both exit my SUV and run to the closed front entrance door of the Big Club.

I try to open the front door and it's locked.

Someone yells from inside, "Who is it?"

"It's me Ryan! Lauren and Ryan!"

The door opens and two guards from the Warriors are standing there.

"Hey Ryan. Sorry for locking you out," says the guard.

Lauren and I walk into the Big Club and the guard shuts the metal front door.

Lauren looks at the guard and says, "I'm Lauren. I'm Ryan's wife."

The guard says, "I know who you are. Nice to meet you. I'm Jakobe and this is Wesley."

"Nice to meet you guys. How are things going here? Are we all secure and running mostly on solar power?"

Jakobe replies, "Yes sir. We are all secure and safe. The solar power is going strong. We have a lot of things running on the solar panels. Just need a couple more panels to run the ovens and freezers."

Lauren and I walk to the center of the Big Club.

I look down at the spot where Joseph's dead body was. The concrete is clean now, but I can picture Joseph's dead body with the white sheet over him.

I turn towards Jakobe and Wesley and say, "I am expecting a woman to come here. She should be coming alone but she might be with another person. Her name is Kat. She shouldn't be a threat but be cautious with her."

Wesley asks, "What time should we expect her?"

"Around 10:30. What time you got now?"

Jakobe looks at his watch and says, "8:33."

I look at my watch and say, "I got 8:35, but that's close enough."

I look at Jakobe and say, "Keep guard at the front and let me know when she arrives. Thank you, Jakobe and Wesley. Nice to meet you guys."

Lauren and I walk around the Big Club.

Lauren grabs a shopping cart and says, "I'm going to bring back a couple of things for myself, Lisa, Kylie, Ann, Nicole, and the babies. The girls could use a couple items from here."

I walk towards the rear entrance and say, "Okay sweetie. Take whatever you want. I'm going to check out the back entrance over here."

Lauren walks down an aisle and starts looking at some items in the health and wellness section of the store.

The store is clean, secure, and well-lit now.

William's group is doing a good job protecting and maintaining the store.

I walk to the back entrance of the store and over to the two Warrior guards.

"Hey guys. I'm Ryan."

The woman and man look at me and reply, "Hey Ryan. How are you?"

I look at the new metal door that was installed and say, "I'm pretty good. How are things here? Any problems? What are your names?"

The woman answers, "I'm Hailee and this is Donnie. The store has been very good. No problems. Only a couple of people have come by the store looking for help. We are still giving out the care packages, but there haven't been too many people coming by lately."

I look at Donnie and ask, "Can you please open the door?"

Donnie replies, "Yes sir."

Donnie unlocks the rear door and pushes open the heavy thick metal door.

Rain is coming down as Donnie opens the door.

I walk to the doorway and look out.

The rear entrance is heavily secured now. Huge piles of large truck tires surround the rear entrance and are blocking any zombie, person, or vehicle from getting in.

I look at Donnie and ask, "What's that wood platform next to the tires?"

Donnie walks over to me and says, "That's a lookout platform. The tires make it hard to see into the streets. The platform will give us some sight lines. It's not finished yet. It's been raining too much lately. When the rain clears, we will finish the platform and secure it."

"Nice. It looks great guys. I see you have the roof

ladder inside the tire border, so we can safely get up to the roof. Have you noticed any leaks from the roof?"

Hailee responds, "No leaks or problems just yet. We will keep an eye on it though. How is everything back at Citrus Oaks and at Warrior High?"

Donnie and I close the heavy rear entrance door.

I look at Hailee and say, "Everything is pretty good now. I haven't been to your home at Warrior High lately, but I haven't heard about any problems."

Donnie says, "Good. I hope those teenage punks don't come around our home anymore. That one kid is a pain in the butt. I wish my brother let me take care of him."

Hailee says, "Baby, those kids are nothing but trouble. The one teenage group is good, but that one group is a major pain in the ass. I wish William would let us take them out. I was never that bad when I was in high school."

I don't know what Donnie and Hailee are talking about, but I'm very interested in their conversation.

"Who is your brother Donnie? What's up with the bad teenagers?"

Donnie says, "I am Tran's brother. He's the car guy for William. Bruce is our uncle. At least that's what Tran tells me."

Hailee says, "The teenagers we were talking about are a pain in the ass. There seems to be several groups of teenagers, almost like gangs. Rivals from different high schools. Most of them aren't bad and are looking for help, but the one group led by this punk kid Dolan are definitely a problem."

"Remember that time they tried to get into the school and steal a car. That Dolan kid needs to go. He has to be the one causing most of the vandalism and problems

46

at the Eastern part of the school," says Donnie.

Lauren shouts, "Honey! Can you help me with this thing?"

"I'll be right there!"

I look at Donnie and Hailee and say, "Nice to meet you two. I want to know more about those problem teenagers. I'll talk to you later."

I walk over to Lauren.

Lauren is trying to pick up a heavy coffee maker box that is stuck on a high shelf.

Lauren is only 5 feet 3 inches tall and is struggling to reach the box.

I grab the box and place it in her cart.

"Can you get me two of them?" asks Lauren.

I grab another coffee maker and stack it on top of the other coffee maker that I just put in Lauren's cart.

"What's up with the coffee makers?"

"Nicole and Lisa were talking about how they missed coffee. I know we have tons of those coffee cup things for this coffee maker. I just thought it would be nice to give them each one," says Lauren.

I grab a nearby shopping cart and put one of the coffee makers from Lauren's cart in my cart.

"What else did you get?"

Lauren replies, "Just a couple of woman products for the girls. Lisa has been having a tough time lately. I know she misses her home in North Carolina. I got a couple of things for her to try and make her feel more at home."

"That's a good idea. Let's take these items and load them into our SUV. It's right around 10:30 now. I'm sure Kat will be here any minute now."

Lauren and I exit the Big Club through the front

entrance and load the items Lauren picked out into my SUV trunk.

The rain has become a very light drizzle and the sun has started to come out.

"It's so hot outside," says Lauren as we walk back into the Big Club.

About an hour goes by and Kat still hasn't made it to the store.

I look down at my watch and Lauren sees that I'm concerned about the time.

Lauren says, "I think I hear a vehicle pulling up."

I walk over to the closed front door next to Jakobe and Wesley.

I hear two car doors open and then close.

Wesley says, "Sounds like two of them. We never open the door for anyone. They have to knock, and we usually have the metal fencing closed at the front entrance before you can get to the front door."

I can hear a woman and a man talking. The voices are muffled as I'm listening through the closed metal door, but I can hear two people talking.

There is a light knock on the metal door.

Knock! Knock!

"Who is it? What do you want?" asks Jakobe.

"It's Kat and Brian. We are here to see Ryan," says Kat.

Jakobe looks at me and asks, "Kat and Brian? Should we let them in?"

I look at Jakobe and Wesley, "Yeah. Let them in but keep your guns on them. We have to check them first. Trust is earned."

Wesley opens the door and Jakobe points his rifle at Kat and Brian.

"What the hell? We mean no harm! I have an appointment with Ryan!" shouts Kat as she stands outside the front entrance of the Big Club next to Brian.

I walk next to Jakobe and say, "Come in Kat and Brian. We need to check you first before we show you around. We are just being safe with everything. Safety first and always."

Jakobe and Wesley escort Kat and Brian in the store. I close the front entrance door and lock it.

"I'm sorry we are late, but The Grove can be hectic at times. Brian and I couldn't get away from our patients," says Kat.

"What weapons do you have on you?" asks Wesley.

Kat and Brian show Jakobe, Wesley, and me their weapons.

"Place your weapons on the table at the front of the store. You will get your weapons back when we are done. No one will touch your weapons while you are here."

Kat gives me an unsure look.

Brian says, "No problem Ryan. We mean no harm."

Lauren asks, "What's The Grove?"

Kat puts her weapons on the table and says, "It's the old baseball stadium in St. Petersburg. It was turned into a FEMA camp, shelter, and makeshift hospital. Brian and I are nurses there."

Brian and Kat put all their weapons on the table at the front of the store and show us that they don't have any weapons on them now.

"I'm sorry about the weapons, but we need to be safe. We have had some trouble in here in the past and we are just being cautious with things."

Kat says, "I understand. We have our security at The Grove as well."

Brian looks at our huge warehouse and says, "Man, you guys have so much stuff here. You'll be good for generations in here."

"Come on guys, grab a shopping cart and let's see what you guys want from this place."

Kat grabs a shopping cart and says, "Again, I'm sorry we were late. I know I didn't mention Brian at World of Trade, but he's a good guy and I needed his car. My car is out of gas."

Brian walks over to Kat with a shopping cart and says, "Only used me for a ride huh? Real nice Kat."

Kat says, "You know what I mean Brian."

"That's okay. I understand. Just try to be on time next time and don't bring tons of people here. Our supplies need to last a long time. We aren't running a charity here."

Kat looks down an aisle and asks, "What are you running here? Why did you even let us in?"

I stop walking and look at Kat.

"We are helping people here, but I just want to make it known that we aren't just giving everything away here. I want to help people, but I have learned in my life not to be a sucker and just give things away for free."

Brian says, "I understand what you are saying Ryan. You don't want to get taken advantage off, especially when you are helping people. I get it."

Kat says, "I agree with you Ryan. I'm just trying to figure out our agreement and what you want from this deal."

I think about what Kat says and I'm not sure what I want from Kat and Brian. I believe in karma and the principle that you get what you give in this world. I do enjoy helping others succeed in life.

"I just want to help you and form an alliance with

you. You were looking for household items like soap, shampoo, deodorant, and stuff we have an abundance of here. What can you offer us in return?"

Kat says, "That's my point. I'm not sure what we can provide you. You already have all this. What else do you need?"

Lauren says, "Material positions aren't everything. These products are great and will help us, but people are what the world needs. Good people. Good people to get rid of the bad people, problems, and zombies."

I look at Lauren and nod my head.

"Well said Lauren. I agree with what she said."

Brian sees a box on a shelf and shouts, "No way! I can't believe you have this here!"

Brian walks over to a box in the electronic aisle.

I walk over to Brian and ask, "What is it?"

"It's a drone. A super expensive drone. I have a drone with a crappy camera on it. This one here is awesome. The battery lasts days before a recharge. The camera works at night, you can go super high with this drone, and the zoom on the camera is awesome," says Brian.

"Well, you can have it. Take two actually. We have about 30 of them here."

"You serious? That's awesome. Thank you," says Brian.

"You'll have to show me how to use one of these things. I have never used a drone before."

Kat and Lauren walk down the health and wellness section.

Kat grabs a couple bottles of shampoo from a shelf and looks at Lauren.

Lauren looks at Kat and says, "Take what you

would like to have, just don't clear out any shelves or anything. I'll let you know if you can't have something."

Kat smiles and says, "Thank you. You and Ryan are awesome for this. The people at The Grove will be very thankful for these supplies."

Kat grabs some vitamins, soap, toothpaste, tooth brushes, protein bars, and laundry detergent.

"So, you are getting supplies for the FEMA camp at The Grove?" asks Lauren.

Kat says, "Yeah. My friends and I started working at The Grove about a month ago. FEMA came in some time ago and set up camps and shelters around Tampa Bay. They are at The Grove, the football stadium, and a couple other locations around here and in the state of Florida."

"I don't remember the baseball stadium being called The Grove since the team left here. I guess FEMA set up shelters last year from the bad hurricane season and never left?" asks Lauren.

Kat and Lauren walk towards the front of the store.

"Yeah. Luckily, FEMA already had somewhat of a presence here from last year's hurricane season. It was pretty bad last year on the West Coast of Florida. The West Coast had some close calls with storms," says Kat.

"Is Brian your boyfriend?" asks Lauren.

Kat replies, "No. He's just a friend. My husband didn't make it. I lost my husband at the start of the craziness around here. My husband was swarmed by a group of zombies. I really hope he isn't a zombie aimlessly walking around Tampa Bay."

Brian and I load up two shopping carts and make it back to the front of the store where Lauren and Kat are standing.

Lauren looks at me and says, "Kat and Brian are

nurses at the FEMA camp at The Grove. They are taking most of these items for the people at the shelter."

"Yeah, Brian told me that also. Do you guys still have room at The Grove?"

Kat says, "Yeah. We have a lot of room at The Grove for people. I think the football stadium has some room also."

"Good, because we get people coming here looking for help, and we can direct them to the baseball stadium now."

Kat says, "Yeah. We can take people in still. We take people in all the time. We just had a large group of people come in from Naples, Sarasota, Fort Lauderdale, and Boca."

Lauren looks at me when she hears Kat say Boca.

"I'm interested in seeing The Grove. Can Lauren and I see where you work?"

Brian says, "Yeah. We can always use some extra hands and another doctor."

Lauren smiles and looks at me.

Kat asks, "Okay, what's the damage here? What do we owe you for all this?"

I look at the stuff that Brian and Kat have in their shopping carts and don't see any high priced or rare items besides the expensive drones.

"The deal is that Brian shows me how to use the drone and you let us in The Grove with VIP status."

Brian says, "I'll show you how to use the drone for sure. When you come by The Gove, I will show you how to use it."

Kat smiles and asks, "That's it? What's the catch?"

I laugh and say, "No catch. Just want to know some information about The Grove, FEMA, and everything going on around here. I'll even bring a bunch more supplies for you when we come by."

Kat says, "Great. Come by any time. Brian and I live there. I will introduce you to the doctors and the people in charge at The Grove."

I look at Kat and Brian and say, "Great. Let's get you all loaded up."

Kat, Brian, Lauren, Wesley, Jakobe, and myself go outside of the Big Club and over to Brian's car.

The sunshine is out, and the sky is clear.

We load up Brian's car with all the supplies.

Wesley and Jakobe take the shopping carts.

Lauren, Kat, Brian, and myself go back into the Big Club and over to the front table where Kat and Brian's weapons are.

Brian and Kat grab their weapons and make sure they didn't forget anything.

"I'm looking forward to learning about the drone Brian."

Brian replies, "Me too. The drone you gave me will really help out. St. Petersburg is having a lot of trouble still. The drone will help me get visuals on the trouble areas while I'm safely inside the protected borders of The Grove."

Lauren asks, "St. Pete is bad? What's going on there?"

Kat puts her handgun in her holster and says, "St. Pete is rough. Downtown St. Pete is a war zone. It's filled with zombies, gangs, dead bodies, and more and more gunfire. The pier is a battleground and most streets are unsafe to even walk down."

"I want to know more about St. Pete and what's going on down there. Tampa Bay is important to me and that includes St. Pete."

I see that Brian and Kat aren't wearing orange badges like Lauren and I are.

"Has anyone given you orange badges?"

Brian and Kat say, "No."

"I will bring some badges with me when I see you at The Grove."

"What's up with the badges?" asks Brian.

"The orange badges are supposed to protect people from being killed by the military. If you don't have a badge when the military sees you, they might kill you."

"How do you know this?" asks Kat.

"People around the area have told us this. I trust the information and it's not worth the risk to not have a badge that could save your life."

"Then we need those badges. Please bring some badges for us when you make it to The Grove. When do you plan on coming by?" asks Kat.

I look at Lauren and say, "Tomorrow, we will come by. We are interested in checking out St. Pete and The Grove."

Kat says, "Great. I will tell my boss to expect you some time tomorrow."

"We will be there around noon or so tomorrow."

"Sounds good. Thank you, Ryan and Lauren," says Kat.

Lauren and I say goodbye to Brian and Kat as they exit the Big Club.

Lauren looks at me and asks, "People from Boca at The Grove? My parents could be there?"

I look at Lauren and say, "Maybe sweetie. Hopefully. We will check it out tomorrow."

CHAPTER 5
TO THE GROVE

"You ready to go Lauren?"

"I'll be right out. I'll meet you and Phil outside," says Lauren.

Phil and I exit my house.

"What's up with this place? The Grove? Why is it called that?" asks Phil.

I put my gear, katana, the orange badges, and two bags in the trunk of my SUV.

"It's called The Grove, because of some orange juice company took over the naming rights to the baseball stadium after the team left. The Grove is basically a FEMA shelter now. People go there for medical care, safety, food, and help. I'm sure we will see some people in pretty rough shape there."

Phil says, "I have been wondering how people are making out since the world fell apart. I'm sure The Grove will be an eye-opening place."

Lauren comes out of our house and locks the front door.

"Hey Phil. What's going on?" asks Lauren.

Phil says, "Ready to roll to the Big Club and then to The Grove."

Lauren puts her bow, bolts, and bags into the back of the SUV next to Phil's gear, shotgun, and bags.

"Let's get going."

Lauren, Phil, and I get into my SUV.

I start up my SUV and look at Lauren.

"You got everything?"

Lauren says, "I got everything I need. Let's go. I'm anxious to get going."

I exit out of my driveway and exit the neighborhood through the South entrance.

Phil asks, "Why are you anxious to get to The Grove?"

Lauren looks at me and says, "I'm curious about what goes on there and who is there. Kat told us that they got a bunch of people from all over Florida."

Phil asks, "Who are you looking for Lauren? Who are you hoping is there?"

"My parents mostly. They were living in Boca Raton. Kat said she met some people at The Grove that were from Boca," says Lauren.

I glance at Lauren as I am driving down the road and feel that she is hoping to see her parents at The Grove. I feel that it's a long shot to find her parents, but I want to stay positive for Lauren.

"They definitely could be there sweetie but even if they aren't, we will make a trip to Boca to find them."

Lauren smiles and says, "Thank you honey. That means a lot to me."

I turn down a street and see a small SUV stopped at the edge of the road in the distance.

A woman is flagging me down to stop.

Lauren says, "That woman wants you to stop. Are you going to stop and help them?"

Phil says, "Slow down, but don't stop completely. Let's check this out before we just blindly help them."

I agree with Phil and slow down as I approach the

woman and the SUV.

The woman shouts with an European accent, "Please! Help us!"

The woman is holding a little white poodle in her hands.

I drive past the SUV and off to the side of the road.

Phil, Lauren, and I look around to see if it is a trap and what is going on around the SUV and the woman.

"The coast is clear right now. I see a man working on the engine. I think they are just broken down," says Phil.

Lauren looks at me and asks, "What should we do?"

I look at Lauren and say, "Stay near the SUV and cover Phil and me. Phil and I will check out these people."

Phil, Lauren, and I exit my SUV.

The woman comes running over to me and says, "Thank you. Thank you. We need your help. Our vehicle just broke down."

Phil says, "No problem ma'am. Where were you headed?"

The man stands up from leaning under the hood of his SUV and shouts something in another language.

The woman says, "We were going to St. Petersburg to the shelter. We ran out of food in the house we were renting for the summer. We are from Belgium."

Phil walks over to the man and says, "Hello sir. I'm Phil. You mind if I take a look at your SUV?"

The man shouts, "Go ahead! The belt keeps slipping off!"

I look at the woman and ask, "What's your name ma'am?"

The woman replies, "I am Tamara. That's my husband Jan, and this is our dog Luna."

"Very cute ma'am. Your dog is very cute. How long have you been stuck here?"

I look over at Phil and at the SUV engine.

Tamara says, "I don't know. We have been here about an hour now."

Jan says, "We need to find another vehicle. This one sucks."

Luna barks at something behind the broken-down SUV and we all look that direction.

Four zombies are approaching the vehicle from a nearby neighborhood entrance street.

Lauren runs to the trunk of my SUV and opens the trunk.

I look at Lauren and shout, "Throw me my katana!"

Lauren grabs my katana and tosses it to me.

Phil takes out his handgun and points it at the zombies.

Phil aims his handgun at a zombie, but a body comes running into his view of the zombies.

It's Jan.

Jan takes a tire iron and hits two zombies.

A zombie is about to bite Jan on his neck.

SCHAFF!

An arrow comes flying into the zombies' head before it can bite Jan.

Three more zombies come slowly walking towards Jan's SUV.

Phil kills a zombie with a clean headshot.

BANG!

"Jan come back here!" shouts Tamara as she holds her dog Luna.

I run towards the three remaining zombies and kill them with hacks, slashes, and stabs from my katana.

I look around and see the two zombies that Jan hit with his tire iron.

The two zombies are slowly crawling towards the SUV still.

I walk over to the zombies and stab them both in the back of the head.

The streets and area are clear of zombies now.

Tamara looks at her husband Jan and shouts, "What were you thinking? Always trying to be a hero! You are lucky these people came and helped you!"

Phil and I walk back to Jan's SUV.

Phil grabs the loose alternator belt and tries to put it back on.

I look at Lauren and ask, "You okay?"

Lauren gives me a nod and says, "I'm okay."

Lauren walks past me and grabs the bolt out of the zombies' head.

"Nice shot," says Tamara.

Phil gets the alternator belt back on and says, "Jan. Start it up."

Jan jumps into the driver seat and starts up his SUV.

The SUV starts up.

The belt squeals as it turns but it stays on.

Phil says, "It looks good for now, but you want to get another ride if you are driving a long distance."

Tamara says, "Thank you. We appreciate it. We are only going a couple of miles down the road to The Grove."

I look at Tamara and say, "We are going to The Grove as well. We will see you there. Drive safe."

Jan says, "Thank you. Come on Tamara, let's get going before we break down again."

Phil closes the hood to Jan's SUV.

Tamara gets in the SUV passenger seat.

Phil and I walk back to my SUV.

Jan drives by us and gives us a goodbye honk from his SUV horn.

Lauren shakes off the zombie brains and blood from the bolt she shot into the zombie.

I place my katana and Lauren's bow in the trunk, and we all get back into my SUV.

I pull up to the Big Club parking lot and see that there are some people banging on the protective fence near the front entrance.

Wesley and Jakobe come out to talk to the five people that are banging on the fence.

I drive my SUV to the front entrance.

Lauren, Phil, and I get out of my SUV.

The five people look at us and then go back to yelling at Wesley and Jakobe.

"We want in your store! We don't want your care packages again! We don't need Aspirin! We need shelter!" shouts one of the men at Wesley.

"Excuse me! Step away from the fence please!"

A man looks at me and shouts, "Fuck you!"

I look at the group standing outside of the Big Club and don't see them holding any weapons.

The five people look to be in rough shape.

"Please, everyone! Step away from the fence! My men can't let you in! We can give you some food and water though!"

A woman shouts, "We don't want your shitty food and water! We want inside the store!"

I step towards the man that cursed at me.

The man looks at me and tries to punch me.

I easily duck out of the way from the man's punch.

I look at the man and shout, "Don't freaking touch

me man!"

I step back, and Phil runs over to me.

I look at Jakobe and Wesley and shout, "Keep the fence closed! They don't get anything from us now!"

The man and woman who previously shouted at me look directly at me.

The man and woman grab small knives from their pockets.

I see the man and woman take out their knives, so I reach for my handgun.

Phil fires a warning shot in the air.

BANG!

The woman and man stop in their tracks, while the three-other people run away from the store.

I take out my handgun and point it at the man.

Phil stands next to me and points his handgun at the woman.

The woman looks at me and says, "Shoot us or don't, but don't play any games with us."

I look directly at the woman and shout, "Get the fuck out of here! Don't ever come back here! My men will kill you, if you come back here!"

Phil says, "Both of you. Get the fuck out of here. Go find another store to bother."

The man and woman are just staring at Phil and me.

I raise my gun above the man and woman and pull the trigger.

BANG!

The man and woman duck down.

Phil shouts, "Get the fuck out of here! Before we kill you!"

The man and woman run away from the front entrance of the Big Club towards the street.

I watch the man and woman run away and then look at Phil.

"What ungrateful pieces of crap!"

"You surprised? Everyone wants everything for themselves. You might be being too nice with this place and giving out the care packages. People will take advantage and see your hospitality as weakness or an opportunity to get more out of you," says Phil.

Wesley and Jakobe open the fence and walk over to Phil and me.

I look at Phil and say, "You probably are right Phil. We need to stop giving people handouts."

Wesley says, "I think we should keep giving out items to people though. We just have to pick and choose who to help."

I look at Wesley and say, "That's easier said than done. Let's develop another plan going forward but we won't be giving out anymore care packages. Let's load the rest of the care packages and the items from the list I made into a truck."

Jakobe asks, "What's going on? Where are you taking these supplies and care packages?"

"I will explain inside. What truck can we take with us?"

Jakobe says, "You can take the red truck. I'll go get it from the back and bring it over here."

Jakobe runs back inside the Big Club to get the truck keys.

Lauren walks over to me with the list of items I want to bring to The Grove.

Lauren hands me the list and we walk inside the store.

Phil asks Wesley, "What was up with those people?

Were they here before?"

Wesley replies, "Yeah. They were here before. The man and woman that came at you are a pain in the ass. They have come here several times. I didn't know what to do."

"If they come back here. You need to make an example of them. People will keep trying to take what we have here, and it won't stop unless we show people that we aren't messing around!"

Wesley says, "Yes sir. We will do our best. I don't know if I can kill them, but I will make sure they know not to mess with us."

Phil says, "You have to be willing to kill them, Wesley. They could hurt you and this place. They won't hesitate to kill you, so you need to not hesitate to kill them."

I see the look of concern on Wesley's face.

I walk over to Wesley and say, "Just keep the fence closed. Don't let anyone near the store entrance and no more care packages for anyone."

Phil asks, "What should we get first for The Grove?"

I hand Phil the list.

Phil looks at the list and says, "Okay. Sounds good. I will get the detergents and cleaning supplies in the very back of the store."

Phil runs to the back of the store.

Wesley asks, "What else is on your list? Where are you taking these supplies?"

"We are taking these supplies to a shelter in St. Pete. It's called The Grove."

"Like the old baseball stadium? That Grove?" asks Wesley.

"Yup. The same place. They turned it into a huge FEMA shelter."

Lauren says, "You can always direct people to The Grove. It sounds like they can take in most people and have a lot of room still. We are going there next, so we will find out what it's all about."

Jakobe comes back in through the front entrance of the Big Club and says, "The red pickup truck is ready for whatever you are putting in it."

Wesley looks at Jakobe and says, "They are going to St. Pete and The Grove with these supplies."

Jakobe says, "Nice. Be careful in St. Pete though. I heard that place is pretty rough. Enrique, Felix, and a couple of other people told me about the chaos they saw around downtown St. Pete."

"Felix is crazy. He loves his double sword thing. He's deadly with that weapon. I saw him kill like 20 zombies with his custom double sword thing," says Wesley.

"I'll make sure to be careful in St. Pete, but I hope to meet this Felix and his badass sword. Let's start loading up all the care packages and then I'll start loading supplies on a couple of pallets."

Wesley and Jakobe gather up the remaining care packages and take them outside to the truck.

Phil comes from the back of the store with Hailee and Donnie.

"Hey Ryan. Hey Lauren," says Hailee.

Lauren and I say hello to Donnie and Hailee.

Phil and Donnie take the supplies that Phil got from the back of the store outside to the truck.

Hailee helps Lauren and I gather up the rest of the supplies.

Several hours go by and we finish loading up the red pickup truck with tons of supplies for The Grove.

Lauren looks at the truck and says, "The people at The Grove are getting some good stuff."

Phil says, "I hope they appreciate it."

I walk back into the Big Club and over to the book and DVD section.

I look at the DVDs and find a movie to watch with Lauren when we have our date night.

Hailee and Donnie walk over to me.

Donnie says, "Hey Ryan. It's been fun looking over this place, but I think Hailee and I will be going back home to Warrior High when William comes by this week."

I look at Donnie and say, "Thank you for your service. You and Hailee have been great. I appreciate your help. I'm sure I will see you around when I come visit William."

Hailee says, "Don't be a stranger. Make sure you say hello when you come to Warrior High."

Hailee gives me a hug.

"I will make sure I say hello when I come by Warrior High. You guys need a cool name for your home. The next time I see you two, I want to know the cool name for your home."

Hailee says, "You got it. We will see you later. Be careful out there."

Hailee and Donnie walk back to the rear entrance door.

I look at them and say, "You too. You two be careful as well."

I walk towards the front of the store and find Phil standing with Lauren, Wesley, and Jakobe.

Phil says, "We are all set and ready to go to The

Grove."

Lauren says, "I gotta pee really quick. I'll be right out."

Lauren runs to the bathroom.

I look at Jakobe and Wesley and say, "I want you guys to keep this place secure but also make sure people know not to mess with this place. If the word spreads that the Big Club is open for looting, then we may be in trouble."

Phil says, "Don't open these doors for anyone other than the Brotherhood or the Warriors."

Wesley and Jakobe say, "Okay. We will. We will lock this place down."

Lauren comes back over to us.

"Much better now. I'm ready to go," says Lauren.

I shake Wesley and Jakobe's hand and say, "Keep up the good work guys. Keep the doors shut but if you run into anyone, direct them to The Grove."

Phil, Lauren, and I say goodbye to Jakobe and Wesley.

I shout goodbye to Donnie and Hailee.

They shout goodbye back to me.

Phil and Lauren exit the Big Club.

Phil gets into the truck driver seat and Lauren gets into the passenger seat of my SUV.

I exit the Big Club and get into my SUV driver seat.

Phil starts up the truck.

I start up my SUV.

Phil drives the truck towards the exit of the Big Club parking lot.

I look at Lauren and ask, "You ready for this?"

Lauren replies, "Yeah. I'm nervous, but I'm ready. I really hope my parents are there. I don't want to have to drive all the way down to Boca."

I drive towards the exit of the Big Club.

Phil makes a left-hand turn.

I make a left-hand turn and follow Phil.

I pick up my walkie-talkie and say, "Phil, I'm going to get in front of you and lead the way."

Phil replies through his walkie-talkie, "Sounds good. I don't want to stop with all these exposed products sitting in the back of the truck. People might start looting the truck if I have to stop."

"No problem. It's only about a 15-mile drive from here. I just hope the roads are clear for us. We should get on the highway and take exit 22," I say over my walkie-talkie to Phil.

Phil replies over his walkie-talkie, "Yes sir. Exit 22 it is. Next stop The Grove."

I pass Phil on his driver side.

Phil jokingly gives me the middle finger as I pass him.

Lauren and I laugh at the sight of Phil's middle finger.

I push down on my SUV gas pedal, look at Lauren, and shout, "To The Grove!"

CHAPTER 6
THE GROVE

"We really need to clean out those litter boxes when we get home. Milo keeps peeing in both litter boxes and his pee stinks so bad," says Lauren.

I laugh and say, "We will honey."

"What's so funny?" asks Lauren.

I'm focused on driving towards The Grove and see a big trash pile of debris and a couple of overturned cars.

I glance at Lauren and say, "I just think it's funny how the world has fallen apart, but the everyday responsibilities are still a thing for us. Milo and the kitty litter. I guess Milo didn't get the memo to stop peeing so much."

Lauren says, "We really need to do something with all the trash around the house and neighborhood. It's starting to smell and attract flies."

I agree with what Lauren is saying, but I'm not sure what to do about the trash.

I look at Lauren and say, "I guess Phil and I will have to steal a garbage truck and start a trash collection service. We could really clean up. No competition."

Lauren laughs and smiles at me.

"But seriously. I will come up with a plan to get rid of the trash around the neighborhood and outside of the neighborhood. I'm sure we can burn some of the trash and we'll have to find a place to dump our trash."

Lauren says, "Thank you babe. You know how sensitive to smells I am. Plus the trash is starting to attract bugs and rodents."

I continue driving towards The Grove and see the large dome shaped building with the large bold letters which reads, "THE GROVE."

Phil asks over the walkie-talkie, "Is that it ahead of us? Is that top part painted orange?"

Lauren grabs the walkie-talkie and says, "Yeah. That's it. It's a former aquarium that was turned into a baseball stadium. It's all covered and hopefully a safe shelter for everyone."

Phil says, "Well alright. Should be secure from the elements around here. The streets around here are pretty rough."

I turn into the main entrance of The Grove and I'm met by armed military personnel.

The main entrance is guarded by tons of armed guards inside the thick metal fencing and guard stations.

The former indoor professional baseball stadium and concert venue has turned into a very secure government run shelter.

I look at the armed guard as he stands at my driver side window. The guard is wearing all black military fatigue attire and so are most of the other armed guards. Most are wearing black fatigues, and some are wearing green fatigues.

"Can we help you sir?" asks one of the armed guards at the main entrance.

I look at the man and say, "We are dropping off supplies and meeting a couple of nurses that work here. It's myself and the truck behind me."

The man says, "We will open the gate, and then pull

into a parking space to the right. We need to check you and your cargo."

The two gunmen open the gate and direct me and Phil to drive through the gate and pull into a parking space.

I pull into a parking space, and Phil parks next to me in the truck from the Big Club.

Two different armed guards tap on our windows and tell us to exit the vehicles.

Lauren, Phil, and I exit our vehicles and stand next to my SUV.

"We have to pat you down and check your vehicles," says the guard.

Phil says, "No problem sir. We understand. You better be checking everyone that comes in here. There are some crazy people in this world."

"Are you one of them sir?" asks a different armed guard as he walks over to Phil.

I look at the guard to see if he's joking, but he is serious.

Phil looks at the guard and says, "No. I'm Phil."

I laugh at Phil's comment.

An armed guard comes over to me and pats me and Lauren down.

"We don't allow weapons inside. You need to leave them in your vehicles," says the guard as he sees the handgun in my right thigh holster."

Phil asks, "Can we take knives inside?"

"No weapons! That means no knives!" shouts the guard that patted down Phil.

Phil, Lauren, and I place our weapons in my SUV.

The guard who patted me down says, "You need to get checked out before you enter the facility."

I look at the man and say, "You just checked us

out."

The guard says, "Heath wise. We need to have you see the doctor or a nurse before you enter. You could be infected, and we can't have you spreading anything."

Lauren asks, "Where do we go for that?"

The guard points to a huge line and says, "That's the line to get in. It looks to be about a four to five hour wait. Just based on the size of the line."

I look at the guard and ask, "Can you call Kat or Brian? They are nurses and they are expecting us. We will get checked out, but we can't wait in that line."

The guard looks at the other guard and asks, "What should we do?"

The one guard looks into Phil's truck and says, "They have some good stuff in here."

I look at the two-armed guards and say, "You help us out and we will help you out, or we can just go home with our goods today."

I look at the guard's name badges and say, "Come on, Mills and Schneider."

Mills grabs his radio and says, "We have a group looking for Kat and Brian down here at gate five. Please advise."

The caller on the radio says, "Hold on. Let me find Kat and see what she says."

Lauren looks at me as we are standing in the hot Florida sun.

I look at Lauren and Lauren gives me a side hug.

Phil looks around the area and sees that the thick metal fencing is protecting the borders of The Grove.

Phil looks at Schneider and asks, "Who runs this place? Who feeds this place? Is it secure?"

Schneider smirks and says, "It's very secure. This

place and the other shelters around Tampa Bay are secure. Our security group and FEMA are making our shelters work. We are helping people."

I look at officer Schneider and ask, "Who runs this place?"

Mills gets a call over the radio.

"Kat will be right down. She is finishing up something and will be right down. You are in gate 5?" asks the female caller over the radio.

Mills says, "Okay. Thank you. Yeah, we are in gate 5."

Mills looks at me and says, "It's your lucky day. Kat is coming for ya. Guess you aren't full of shit."

Phil replies, "What? We definitely aren't full of shit. The big truck full of supplies didn't show you anything about us. We are here to help out."

Schneider reaches into Phil's truck and grabs a bottle of detergent.

Phil looks at Schneider and says, "Enjoy that. You need that. You smell terrible."

Schneider drops the bottle of detergent and walks right up to Phil's face.

"Smart ass huh?" shouts Schneider.

"Hey Ryan! Hey Lauren!" shouts Kat as she walks over to us.

Kat walks to us, looks at Mills and Schneider, and says, "Thank you guys. They are with me. They are good people."

Schneider picks up the detergent and stares at Phil.

"Have a good day," says Phil as he stares back at officer Schneider.

Schneider and Mills leave us and walk back to gate 5.

Kat looks at me and asks, "What happened with those two guards? They threaten you or something?"

"They were just giving us a hard time. They told us that we needed to be checked before we came in and it turned into a little problem."

I introduce Kat to Phil and show Kat the stuff we brought for her.

Kat says, "Looks great guys. Thank you. That is more than enough for us."

I go into my SUV and get something.

Lauren looks at Kat and asks, "We don't have to get checked to go inside, do we?"

Kat says, "Actually you do. It's standard protocol. You don't have to wait in that big line. I will check you out in a separate medical room. Anytime you come here, you need to get checked out. Just make sure to ask for me, Brian, or Dr. Morris."

I close my SUV door and lock my SUV.

BEEP!

The horn beeps, which shows me that the doors are locked.

I hand Kat a bag of orange badges and say, "Here are the badges we talked about. I'm surprised no one has given them to you or at least mentioned them to you."

Kat says, "I guess we aren't a high priority for them."

Phil asks, "What should we do with the stuff we brought in the truck? I don't want the guards taking any more of this stuff."

Kat asks, "Can you drive the truck closer to the building? I can have an unloading team start taking the goods off the truck."

"Yeah. Just tell me where to drive," says Phil.

Kat points to a thick concrete pole near an open area and says, "Park the truck in the shade next to the concrete pole with the yellow stripe on it."

Phil gets into his truck and starts up the engine.

Kat, Lauren, and I start walking towards an entrance of The Grove.

Phil reverses out of the parking space and drives next to the concrete pole with the yellow stripe on it.

Phil parks the truck in the shade and exits the truck.

I walk with Lauren and Kat.

Lauren looks at Kat and says, "Quite an operation you have going on here. Looks to be a good place to be holding up."

Kat looks at The Grove entrance and says, "It's not too bad. It's safe. No zombies have gotten in since I have been here, and it's been pretty good. Only a couple of problems here and there."

We walk over to Phil and Phil asks, "Is this spot okay?"

Kat says, "It's great. Lock the truck though. I don't want anyone stealing your ride."

Phil locks the truck doors.

"Now what?" asks Lauren.

Kat says, "We need to check you out first. Come with me."

Kat escorts Phil, Lauren, and myself into The Grove.

I feel like an athlete as we walk into the indoor baseball stadium and into the locker room.

"I'll check out Lauren first. You two wait out here," says Kat.

Lauren and Kat go into the training room of the baseball stadium.

The lights are on and the fans are working inside the

locker room.

I can't help but to feel like a fan as I'm seeing the empty lockers, sofas, and chairs.

"Man, I wish I made it to the pros. They have it pretty sweet in the major leagues," says Phil as he sits in an oversized leather chair.

I sit in one of the big padded chairs and recline.

"This is the life. It's the simple things that matter right now."

Phil walks over to a water cooler and fills up two cups of water.

Phil brings a cup of water over to me.

I thank Phil for the water and drink the cup of water.

"This place is okay so far. I wonder what the rest of the building looks like?"

"Not this nice I'm sure. It could be tent city or bum row out there," says Phil.

Several minutes go by.

Lauren comes out of the training room.

"I'll take Phil next," says Kat from inside the training room.

"Everything okay?"

Lauren replies, "Yeah, I'm not infected."

I look at Lauren and say, "Well. We might all be infected sweetie."

Lauren looks at me with a concerned look and asks, "You believe that we are all infected?"

"I don't know. We haven't had to deal with someone dying of natural causes or coming back to life after dying without being bit or scratched yet."

Lauren sits down in a leather chair and says, "I guess it doesn't matter, but we have to be careful when people get sick or die. I wonder what Kat and the doctors here know about it."

"I'll see what I can find out, when she checks me out."

Lauren walks over to me and says, "I'll check you out."

Lauren kisses me and then grabs my butt with her left hand.

About ten minutes goes by and Phil exits the training room.

"Come on down, Ryan!" shouts Kat from inside the training room.

I walk into the training room and see Kat sitting next to a medical table.

I was going to be an athletic trainer in college and have spent many days in a training room. The sights and smells of the training room take me back to my college days.

Kat is sitting in a four-wheeled stool.

"Come on over here Ryan. Take off your shirt," says Kat.

I walk over to Kat and take off my red athletic shirt.

Kat looks at my bumps, scars, bruises, and says, "Man, you really took a beating. You feeling okay?"

I look at Kat and say, "I'm alive and that's all that matters. My back is killing me. My left shoulder constantly hurts. My chest hurts still from where I got shot, and I've been hungry since we started dealing with these zombies."

Kat takes my temperature, checks my lungs, checks my vitals, skin, eyes, and blood pressure.

Kat says, "Well, you look pretty good. All things considered. You need to rest Ryan. You need to take it easy for a while. The world needs another doctor and someone like yourself. You might be doing too much."

I put my shirt back on, walk around the training room, and think about what Kat said.

I look at Kat and ask, "What do you know about the virus, the zombies, the infected, and what's going on?"

Kat replies, "It's definitely some sort of zombie virus outbreak situation. I don't know much about the outbreak or where it started, but I do know that it's not good. People are struggling around Tampa Bay and St. Pete is pretty rough. It's a mess right outside of here. My boss Dr. Morris might know more about it though. I'll see if she is around for you to meet with her."

"That would be great. I would like to know more about the virus and how things are going around Tampa Bay and the rest of the world."

Kat says, "I would like to know also, but you three are all good. Let's get out of here, and I'll show you guys around this place."

I exit the training room with Kat and walk over to Lauren and Phil who are sitting in oversized leather recliner chairs.

Phil sees Kat and I walking towards him.

"How'd you get this place and all the stuff in here?" asks Phil.

Kat says, "I don't know. It was like this when we took it over. I guess once the baseball team left this stadium and became a different team altogether, they just left everything here."

"I'm definitely not complaining. I might have to come back here," says Phil.

Kat says, "Okay everyone. I'm going to show you around and hopefully we can meet a couple of doctors and other workers."

Kat picks up her radio and asks, "How's the

unloading of that truck coming?"

A man replies over the radio and says, "It's going good. We are separating the goods to evenly distribute among the sections."

Kat replies, "Okay, great. Keep me posted how it's going."

"I will Kat. Thank you," says the man over the radio.

"Welcome, Leroy," says Kat over the radio.

Kat takes us up a flight of stairs and says, "That's Leroy. He's a good guy. He was the head groundskeeper here and lost his job when the team left."

I walk up the stairs with Kat, Phil, and Lauren.

I step up the last step and am shocked where we are.

Phil runs up the last step and shouts, "No way!"

Kat took us on to the baseball field.

I step onto the baseball field and look around the artificial turf field and then the stands.

Lauren and Phil look around as well.

Lauren looks at Kat and asks, "Kat, do you know where I could find any people that came from South Florida?"

Kat looks at Lauren and asks, "You want someone from the University of South Florida?"

Lauren says, "No. I mean the location in Florida. Specifically, Boca Raton. My parents are from there, and I'm hoping to find them here."

Phil comes over to me and says, "This place is pretty awesome, but the lights are terrible. No sunlight gets in here and this artificial turf isn't a good surface to grow anything on."

Lauren comes running over to me and says, "Kat is taking me to a group of people from Boca. Come on."

I walk with Phil, Lauren, and Kat.

Kat takes us around the baseball field and we see people in tents, cots, and sleeping bags.

A lot of people we see are in bad shape and look to be barely staying alive.

Lauren is looking at the people that we pass and is looking for her parents Fran and Keith.

I see a family of four with a dog.

Phil sees an elderly couple sitting on a cot holding each other.

Kat calls over her radio, "Does anyone know where the new group of South Florida people are? I'm looking for a Fran and Keith."

Lauren intently listens to the radio call by Kat and waits for the response.

I see the areas on the field are broken into sections and the stadium is broken into separate groups of sections.

Phil looks at the club box seats in the stands and the big enclosed area in the center field homerun section.

Still no word over the radio to Kat about Lauren's parents.

Kat gets impatient and calls over her radio again.

Phil looks at me and says, "I wonder who is staying in the primo club box seats on the second level and in center field."

I look at the club box seats and see people are in them.

I take a long look at the club box seats and can tell that the people in the club levels look to be in good shape and are better dressed.

Kat calls over her radio again and asks, "I'm looking for a Fran and Keith from Boca. Brian? Stan? Brittany? Anyone read me?"

"I hear ya. I don't have anyone by that name in my section," says a man to Kat over the radio.

A woman replies over the radio, "I hear ya Kat, but I don't have anyone by those names in my section. I think Brian might though."

Brian replies, "I'll have to check. Come to my section though. We can look together."

Kat takes Phil, Lauren, and I to section eleven.

Brian walks over to Kat and says, "Hey guys. How are ya?"

I introduce Phil to Brian and we walk around Brian's section.

Kat looks at Brian and asks, "How are things today? Anyone causing any problems today?"

Brian replies, "Things are pretty good. Another day in paradise."

Lauren walks down an aisle of people and sees a lone woman sitting on a cot. The woman is sitting by herself and reading a book.

Lauren looks at the petite woman and becomes very interested in talking with her.

Lauren walks directly to the woman and notices the woman's black hair, red polo shirt, jeans, and short stature.

I see Lauren moving quickly towards the woman and I start walking towards her.

The woman senses Lauren walking towards her and looks at Lauren.

Lauren sees the woman's face and starts crying.

"Mom?" asks Lauren.

The woman stands up and starts crying.

Lauren hugs the woman.

I see Lauren hug the woman and I smile.

Lauren looks at me and shouts, "It's my mom! She's

alive!"

I walk over to Lauren's mom Fran and give her a hug.

Fran is a short little Italian woman who stands a mere 4 feet 11 inches tall when she is wearing shoes.

Lauren looks at Fran and asks, "Where is dad?"

I fear that Lauren's father is dead as we only see Fran.

Fran says, "Your father is somewhere around here. He was looking for a hot dog. He figured since we were in a ballpark, they should have hot dogs around here."

CHAPTER 7
THAT SHOULD DO IT

"That should do it! Fire it up Bo!" shouts Barrett as he secures the last screw on a solar panel.

Bo runs inside the supermarket entrance and flips on a light switch.

The supermarket lights turn on.

Nicky, Bo, Darby, and the rest of the Pride cheer at the sight of the lights and power turning on in the supermarket as they stand inside the front entrance of the supermarket.

Barrett comes down from the roof of the supermarket and walks over to Bo.

TJ and Janet look at each other and walk away from the group who is standing inside the supermarket still.

TJ says, "I don't know about Bo and Barrett. I can't get a feel for them. They just killed two men and they don't seem to care about it."

Janet looks at TJ and asks, "How are you holding up? How's your head?"

TJ replies, "I'm okay. I really had no choice to take out Armstrong. After Bo and Barrett took out Roberts and Brimley. I had to do it."

Janet says, "You made the right call. We couldn't risk anyone of those three going back home to tell your dad about this place. The military wants this place and they will kill everyone in here to get it. I know how the people at MacDill operate."

TJ says, "I have to talk with my father about everything. I want to leave here very soon and get back to MacDill."

Janet says, "We will leave ASAP. Let's see if Bo and Barrett are leaving also. We do need a ride home though."

TJ replies, "Yes, we do. Our helicopter ride here was a one-way trip."

Bo and Barrett look at the supermarket and see that the power is on, but the store needs to be thoroughly cleaned.

Barrett looks at Bo and says, "I'm glad you are here brother. I was starting to worry about you. Without me around, how can you take care of our ranch?"

Bo says, "That's a big part why I came looking for ya. I need help at the ranch."

TJ and Janet walk over to Bo and Barrett.

"When are you coming back home?" asks Bo.

Barrett looks at Darby, who is standing and talking with Nicky and Aisha.

"I don't know Bo. I feel like my place is here to protect Darby and her Pride," says Barrett.

TJ looks at Bo and asks, "When do you think we can get out of here Bo?"

Bo looks at TJ and says, "Trying to figure that out now. I reckon it will be very soon."

Janet says, "We need a new ride home is all."

Barrett says, "You can take my truck if you like. Just don't mess it up."

Bo looks at Barrett and shouts, "Why aren't you coming back home? Our animals need you! Betty misses you!"

Barrett smiles and says, "I miss Betty. How is my old girl doing?"

TJ looks at Janet and asks, "Who's Betty?"

Janet replies, "How should I know? These two guys are weird."

Nicky and Darby walk over to Bo and Barrett.

"Thank you, guys. The supermarket looks to be working great. The solar power will really help us," says Darby.

Nicky looks at Bo and asks, "What's your plan now Bo?"

Bo replies, "I'm trying to get back home. My ranch and animals need me. They need Barrett also, but he doesn't want to leave here."

Darby looks at Barrett.

"You should get back home with your brother. Take some time to tend to your animals and ranch. I'm not going anywhere honey bear. We will let you back in. We are secure now," says Darby to Barrett.

Barrett is about to reply, but Darby interrupts him.

"I'm not asking you. I'm telling you. We are set here now. We have tons of stuff to do around here. With cleaning the supermarket and tending to our animals. You go home and bring back some supplies for us," says Darby.

Barrett nods his head yes and says, "Yes, ma'am."

Bo says to Nicky, "Where is my girl Chi Chi? I haven't seen her or any of the other cheetahs."

Nicky says, "She got out. When we were under attack by the hunters, zombies, and other people, some of the animals got out. Chi Chi was one of them."

Barrett looks at Darby with a concerned look.

"That was before the wall went up. Plus, we have

Isiah and his group looking out for us outside of the wall now. We are safe," says Darby.

Bo asks, "So Chi Chi got out of her enclosure and could be anywhere in Florida right now?"

Nicky says, "Yeah. Her and her brothers got out. I hope they are okay."

Aisha comes over and gives TJ, Janet, Bo, and Barrett a bottle of water.

They all thank Aisha for the water.

Janet walks over to the lion outdoor exhibit and sees the lion cub Keanu playing with his mother Taraji while Zeus sleeps in the shade.

TJ walks over to Janet and says, "I hope Odin is doing okay. I miss my boy. He's like my child. I have had him since he was a puppy."

Janet looks at Keanu and says, "I'm sure he is okay. O is tough and smart."

TJ and Janet watch the lions play in the lion exhibit and take in the nice moment with each other.

Keanu tries to pounce on Taraji but he's too small and falls into the grass.

Janet sees a human arm in the lion exhibit and looks at TJ.

"What are you going to tell your father about Armstrong, Brimley, and Roberts?" asks Janet.

TJ looks at Zeus and says, "The truth. Armstrong, Brimley, and Roberts didn't make it. They were taken out during this trip and this place isn't safe for anyone to mess with."

Janet says, "Good idea keeping it vague. I like the idea of keeping this place safe. The world needs a nice place like this."

"How the hell do they feed all these animals?" asks

TJ to Janet.

Nicky walks over to TJ and Janet.

"A lot of the animals we have left are vegetarians. The tricky ones are our lions and leopard. We have to feed them zombie meat at times. We try to keep the zombie meat fresh but sometimes it's from older zombies," says Nicky.

"They don't get sick eating zombie meat?" asks Janet.

"No, actually they are in good health. I was surprised by the animals not getting sick also," says Darby as she walks over to Janet.

"The real problem is with our chimps, orangutans, and gorilla. They don't eat meat and we are running low on a viable food source for them," says Darby.

TJ looks at Darby and asks, "Why keep doing this? It seems like a losing battle?"

"Do you have kids?" asks Darby to TJ.

"No, but I have a dog. He's like my child," replies TJ.

"These animals are my kids. We can't just let them die. I am their mother. Our keepers are there family. We can't just let our animals die. What kind of a person does that?" asks Darby with a stern tone.

Janet replies, "We meant nothing by that. It's just a lot of work is all. We are just wondering how you can keep this up?"

Barrett walks over and says, "With our help and all of us working together."

Darby says, "It's getting tougher every day. Food is getting harder to find. We do need some help with all this."

TJ looks at Darby and says, "I meant no disrespect. I'm just amazed by how this place is holding up."

Bo says, "Maybe we can help. At least a little bit. We have some crops growing at our ranch. We can plant some crops for you. Just tell us what you may need here for the animals. Barrett and I can help ya."

Nicky says, "Thanks baby. That would be sweet of you. I'll start up a list of what we need around here for the animals and this place."

Nicky walks with Bo and Barrett into a zoo indoor snack bar.

TJ walks over to Darby and says, "This place is safe with me. I will tell my father who runs MacDill to avoid this place. You won't have any more helicopters flying in here, but how do we get out of here?"

Darby says, "Thank you. It was a shocker to have a helicopter land here. We have three secret entrances built into the walls that can only be opened from the inside."

Darby, TJ, and Janet walk away from the lion exhibit and down a long walkway in the center of the zoo.

Janet says, "You have an awesome place. I'm glad you are maintaining this place. If we have any chance at rebuilding the world, it starts with places like this."

Darby stops at an empty tiger exhibit.

"We have had our losses though. Luckily, the walls went up fast after the first couple of attacks on this place. I will keep fighting for this place, my Pride, and my animals. I feel my purpose is here," says Darby as she looks into the empty tiger exhibit.

A woman walks over to Darby, TJ, and Janet. The woman is carrying a large box of stuff.

"What should we do with the soldiers' vests, weapons, and gear?" asks the woman.

Darby looks at the box and then at TJ.

TJ says, "Let me see that box."

The woman hands TJ the box and TJ puts the box on the ground.

TJ goes through the box and says, "I will take the name tags of the soldiers and anything else you don't want."

Darby looks at the items in the box and says, "Okay. We can use the weapons though. The guns, the knives, and the grenades will help us protect this place."

Janet says, "You got it. They are all yours."

TJ takes the name tags off the military vests and the woman picks up the box from the ground.

"Put that box in my office Allie," says Darby.

Allie walks away from Darby and towards the zoo offices.

Janet looks at Darby and says, "I'm sorry about Armstrong, Brimley, and Roberts. They weren't with us. They were forced upon us for this trip."

Darby looks at Janet and says, "Thank you. I'm sorry about them as well. I didn't want them to die, but Bo and Barrett thought otherwise."

"They killed them quickly and without hesitation," says TJ.

Darby says, "I don't like killing, but it's part of this world. Bo and Barrett are good guys. They both have that animal instinct to protect their family and will do whatever it takes to protect themselves and their loved ones."

A large group of birds comes flying into the zoo and towards the bird aviary part of the zoo.

Janet and TJ look up at the large amount of birds and are amazed at how they are all flying together.

"What is up with all the birds?" asks Janet.

"They come and go. They were set free by our aviary specialist Mr. Charlie, but they keep coming back here every couple of days," says Darby.

"Is that a pair of owls?" asks Janet.

Darby says, "Yeah. That's PB and Jay. They never leave each other."

"What happened to Mr. Charlie?" asks TJ.

Darby looks at the birds and says, "He's around. He helps guard this place."

Bo, Barrett, and Nicky come over to Darby.

"How'd you make out Nicky?" asks Darby.

"Pretty good. Bo has a plan for bringing some of his crops back here and he'll start planting new crops when he gets back," says Nicky.

Bo looks at Barrett and says, "We will start planting them when we get back home. Right brother?"

Barrett looks at Darby with a sad look.

Darby walks over to Barrett and gives him a kiss.

"We will be safe honey bear. Don't worry about us. The crops will help us here. We need them," says Darby.

Aisha comes running over to Darby.

"We have another problem with Louie," says Aisha.

Darby and Nicky run with Aisha into the primate sanctuary building.

TJ looks at Janet and says, "I want to see this."

Janet and TJ run to the primate sanctuary building while Bo and Barrett stand outside.

TJ and Janet enter the primate sanctuary building and find it dimly lit.

The loud bang of something slamming into the ground is heard in the distance.

BANG!

"Stop that Louie!" shouts Darby.

Janet and TJ walk towards the back of the building where Aisha, Darby, and Nicky are standing.

"How long has he been doing this?" asks Darby to Aisha.

Aisha replies, "He's been doing this more often since Mo died. He hasn't been the same since Mo died."

Janet and TJ walk to the back section of the building and find a large silver back gorilla looking at Darby through the large floor to ceiling glass window.

Louie is a large silver back gorilla.

Louie runs towards the glass and punches the window.

TJ steps back as Louie punches the window.

"Don't worry, the window won't break. It's reinforced glass with unbreakable polymers in it," says Nicky as she looks at TJ.

Janet asks, "Who was Mo?"

Darby looks at Louie, who know has his back to Darby, and says, "It was his gorilla girlfriend. She recently got sick and we had to put her down."

Aisha says, "Louie and Mo grew up together. He's heartbroken."

Janet feels bad for Louie and walks over to the glass.

Janet puts her hand on the glass.

Louie turns around and walks towards Janet.

TJ gets nervous for Janet.

Louie slowly walks towards Janet and sits down.

Louie looks at Janet and makes eye contact with her.

Janet whispers, "It's okay. We will find you a new friend."

Louie slowly reaches for the glass and puts his hand on the glass where Janet's hand is.

Janet smiles at Louie.

Janet says, "Stay strong Louie. Everything will be okay."

91

Janet takes her hand away from the glass.

Louie gets mad.

Louie runs away from the glass and towards the back of his indoor enclosure.

Nicky looks at Janet and says, "Louie likes you. I haven't seen him like that in a long time."

Janet walks over to TJ.

Darby looks at Aisha and says, "Let Louie outside today. We really need to clean his enclosure."

Aisha says, "I will let him out in a couple of minutes and we will clean his enclosure."

"Thank you, Aisha," says Darby.

TJ and Janet exit the primate sanctuary and find Bo and Barrett sitting in the shade.

"You ready to get going or what?" asks Bo.

TJ replies, "Yes sir. I'm ready to get back to MacDill and my house."

Bo says, "Okay then. We'll get going shortly. Just have to figure out who is coming with us."

Nicky and Darby exit the primate sanctuary building.

Bo shouts, "Nicky, you coming with us?"

"Where you going?" asks Nicky.

"Home. Home on the ranch. Where my horses and my cows roam," sings Bo.

Nicky replies, "Not this trip baby. I have to do some things here before I leave. I'll be back to my house and then your ranch in a couple of days though."

Barrett looks at Darby and asks, "What about you Darby? You ever leaving this place?"

Darby looks at Barrett and replies, "Someday I'll leave, but not today. We got too much going on around here."

TJ looks at Darby and says, "I just want to get our weapons and belongings from your office Darby."

Darby says, "Go ahead. We'll meet you guys right back here."

Janet and TJ walk to Darby's office and get their belongings.

Nicky, Darby, Bo, and Barrett talk.

"You got a good thing going on here Miss Darby," says Bo.

Darby punches Bo in the shoulder and says, "No thanks to you though. Why are you bringing other people around here?"

Bo replies, "What? Janet and TJ are good people. Those other three soldiers weren't with us."

Barrett says, "Just be more careful with bringing people around here and to the ranch. Be smarter with your decisions."

Bo looks at Barrett and says, "If you didn't just leave one morning without telling me what your plan was, then I wouldn't have to go all over the place looking for you."

Barrett says, "Sorry about that. I was just worried about Darby is all. My nerves got the best of me."

Darby looks at Bo and Barrett and says, "Enough you two. Just don't be bringing everyone here. This is our home. We already fought off a large group to keep this place safe. We don't need another battle in here."

"Yes ma'am. We won't let that happen," says Barrett.

Bo replies, "I'm sorry Darby. I won't let anything happen to this place."

Nicky says, "We should be fine now. We have Isiah and his group watching this place, and Mr. Charlie also has eyes on this place."

Darby says, "We are good for now, but it only takes one wrong decision to destroy this place. We have come to far to mess this up."

Janet and TJ come walking back over to Darby, Nicky, Barrett, and Bo.

"All ready to go?" asks Janet.

Bo says, "Yes ma'am. Just need Darby and Nicky to show us how to get out of here."

Darby says, "Follow me."

Darby and Nicky take TJ, Janet, Bo, and Barrett towards the back of the property.

"Where is your truck Barrett?" asks Nicky.

Barrett replies, "I'm not sure."

Bo says, "I saw your truck, Barrett. It's right outside the wall on the East part of the property."

Nicky asks, "You sure? When was that?"

"A couple of days ago. Didn't you hear the gunfire and big explosion a couple of days ago?" asks Bo.

Darby says, "We hear explosions, gunfire, and screams all the time."

Darby and Nicky take TJ, Janet, Bo, and Barrett towards the East part of the property.

The zoo is at the Southern part of the property, the supermarket and shopping center are at the Northern part, and homes are at the East and West parts of the property.

Nicky points to a large metal door.

The metal door is secured to strong thick concrete walls.

"Remember, once you leave this place, you can only get in by one of our hidden entrances. There is no handle outside or clear markings to an entrance. The doors are covered with objects and debris to blend in with the other

94

parts of the wall," says Nicky.

"How can we get back in?" asks Barrett.

Darby hands Barrett something and says, "Take this duck whistle and blow it three times near one of the entrances."

"How will I know where the entrance is?" asks Barrett.

Darby says, "We put a sign at each entrance, plus an X will be written on the center of the door. The sign on this entrance should read, DO NOT ENTER LIONS WILL EAT YOU."

TJ and Janet get their guns ready.

Barrett and Bo hug Darby and Nicky.

"I will see you again honey bear," says Darby to Barrett.

Nicky kisses Bo and says, "See you soon baby. I'll come by your ranch in a couple of days."

Darby looks at TJ and Janet and says, "Nice to meet you TJ and Janet. Take care."

TJ and Janet say goodbye to Darby and Nicky.

Nicky opens the large metal exit door slightly.

"The coast is clear. Be safe everyone," says Nicky as she opens the metal door a little more.

TJ, Janet, Bo, and Barrett run out the exit.

Darby and Nicky close the metal door.

Bo says, "There is your truck Barrett."

Barrett and Bo get into the truck, followed by TJ and Janet.

Barrett starts up his truck and asks, "Where are we going?"

TJ says, "To MacDill Air Force Base. I have to get my jeep and talk with my father."

CHAPTER 8
ST. PETE

"They don't have anything around here!" shouts Lauren's father Keith as he sits down next to Lauren's mother Fran.

"Hey dad," says Lauren.

Keith looks at Lauren and says, "Hello. How are you?"

Keith hugs Lauren.

"Where is Ryan?" asks Keith.

"Hey Keith," I say to Keith as he hugs Lauren.

Keith shakes my hand.

"How are you doing Keith?"

Keith looks at me and says, "We are doing okay. We lost some people, but we are making it."

Lauren looks at Fran and asks, "What happened to Melania, Lainey, grandma, Aunt Ruth, and Uncle Todd?"

Fran replies, "Grandma, Melania, and Lainey didn't make it. They were gone pretty quickly. Your Aunt Ruth and Uncle Todd could still be alive."

"What happened with them?" asks Lauren.

Fran says, "They were going to The Villages near Ocala and we haven't seen them since. They ran out of food and left their home in Boca for The Villages. Aunt Ruth wanted to try her luck with Aunt Jessica at The Villages."

"Good luck with that. There are so many people at

The Villages. That place must be crawling with zombies now," says Keith.

I look at Keith and ask, "How long have you guys been here?"

Keith replies, "I don't know. What's today?"

Lauren replies, "I have no idea what day it is."

"Me either."

Keith says, "I really don't know how many days we have been here. It could be close to a week now."

"How did you get here?"

"We were leaving Boca to either go to Orlando or Tampa. We planned on coming to see you guys or a friend of ours who lives in Orlando. Fran picked Tampa to see Lauren. During the drive here, our car broke down," says Keith.

"Is your car okay?"

Keith replies, "We got a flat tire. When I was trying to fix it, I hurt my shoulder fighting off a group of zombies."

"Did you get bit or scratched?" asks Lauren.

"No. I didn't get touched by a zombie. I killed a couple of zombies before a car came and helped us. We killed the zombies, but my shoulder was injured," says Keith.

Fran says, "I had to drive us here. The people in the car helped us put the spare tire on the car and told us about this place."

"That was lucky. I'm glad you guys are safe. I was worried sick about you," says Lauren.

"What did they say about your shoulder Keith?"

Keith replies, "They don't know. They suck here. It could be a torn rotator cuff."

"We are going to get you out of here and to our

house today," says Lauren.

Brian walks over to me.

"Can I talk with you for a second?" asks Brian.

I excuse myself from Lauren, Fran, and Keith.

"What's up Brian?"

"Two things actually. Keith is a diabetic and he really needs his insulin. I got you two pens of insulin, but that's all I could get," says Brian.

"Thank you, Brian. I appreciate it. Insulin is going to be tough to find."

"The other thing is that we are having some trouble with the local area of St. Pete. I was wondering if you could help us out. The guards won't leave their stations and don't really do much around here. I'm worried about this place," says Brian.

"I'm not set up for taking on zombies today, but I can come back another time with my team."

Brian says, "That would be great. Today, I want to show you the streets of St. Pete with the drone you gave me. It's pretty awesome. We can stay inside the fence of The Grove and send out the drone to show us what's going on in St. Pete."

"Phil and I will help you if you can take care of Keith, Fran, and Lauren until we leave."

Brian replies, "No problem. Whatever they need."

"Where is Phil anyway?"

Brian replies, "I think he is with Kat. They were going to see if they could meet Dr. Morris. I'll call Kat over the radio."

I walk over to Lauren and talk with her.

"I'm going to go with Brian for a second. He wants me to check out the streets of St. Pete and hopefully I can meet the head doctor here, Dr. Morris."

Lauren asks, "You are going outside?"

"We are using the drone to see the streets of St. Pete. I'll be outside but not outside of the fence. I will be safe."

Lauren says, "Okay, I'll wait here with Fran and Keith. I love you."

I kiss Lauren.

A little girl watches me kiss Lauren and smiles as she plays with her little doll in the tent next to Fran and Keith.

Brian walks over to me and says, "Kat is with Phil at Dr. Morris' office. We will go there right now, then go outside with the drone."

"Who will take care of these people while you are gone?"

"Felicia and Cami will take over my section while I'm gone with you," says Brian.

"Okay great."

I say goodbye to Lauren, Fran, Keith, and the little girl who watched me kiss Lauren.

Brian takes me to the big enclosed premium luxury box section that is located in the center part of the outfield seats at The Grove.

I walk up the steps with Brian and am nervous to meet with Dr. Morris.

Brian opens the door to a luxury box, I see Phil and Kat talking with a woman in a white lab coat.

"Hey Ryan," says Kat.

"Hey everyone."

Phil asks, "Everything okay?"

"Yeah, everything is good. Lauren's parents are here and safe."

"Very cool," says Phil.

Kat introduces me to Dr. Morris.

Dr. Morris is sitting in a leather computer chair at a large desk in the center of the room. The room is very big and has several large floor to ceiling windows that look directly on to the baseball field.

Dr. Morris is a tall olive skinned skinny woman that has long brunette hair tied back into a ponytail.

"Nice to meet you Ryan. Kat was telling me about you. You are an orthopedic doctor? A surgeon?" asks Dr. Morris.

"Yes, Dr. Morris. I."

"Please. Call me Jenna," interrupts Dr. Morris.

"Sorry. Jenna. I'm an orthopedic surgeon. I worked at Tampa Hospital for the past 10 years."

"Impressive. We could use a man with your talents around here," says Jenna.

"Thank you, but I can't commit to a job right now. I'm trying to get a hold of things in this new world and protecting my family and my group are my priorities."

Kat interrupts, "Ryan is the leader of a group in Tampa. He has some connections in this new world and should be very helpful for us."

Jenna says, "Great. I'm sure Ryan and Phil will be great additions around here."

I look at Phil and say, "We aren't staying here. Jenna. I was just dropping off some supplies and checking out your facility."

Jenna takes off her white lab coat and puts it on the back of her leather computer chair.

"Like anything you see?" asks Jenna with a seductive tone.

"Your place is very nice. You have a nice operation here."

"Thank you, Ryan," says Jenna as she looks out the

big glass window onto the baseball field that is filled with people, tents, and cots.

"I was wondering if you could tell me anything about the zombie virus, how things are looking in the U.S., and really any pertinent information?"

"I would love to talk with you about things and the state of the world. When would you be available to discuss things?" asks Jenna.

"How about right now?"

Jenna turns around from the window and looks at her desk.

Jenna says, "Unfortunately, I can't right now. I would love to talk over dinner some time."

Kat says, "Ryan, is just looking for some answers and not some big meeting, Jenna."

Jenna glares at Kat and shouts, "It's Dr. Morris! Kat!"

Kat apologies to Dr. Morris.

"I would just love to have a nice conversation with a fellow doctor about things. We can discuss what we both want in this world and what we know about this world," says Jenna.

"I'll meet with you Dr. Morris," says Phil.

Jenna replies, "Thank you, Phil, but Ryan and I can discuss medical topics that you probably won't understand."

Jenna takes her brunette hair out of her ponytail and lets her hair down.

I feel awkward with the tone and sexual nature of Jenna.

I try to diffuse the situation, but I don't know how to talk with Dr. Morris.

Dr. Morris is a very attractive woman, but I could

never cheat on Lauren. Lauren is my soulmate and I would never want to hurt her.

Jenna picks up a pencil from her desk and says, "Well, let me know when you can meet with me Ryan. I'll pencil you in."

"I will. Thank you for your time Jenna."

I quickly exit the room with Brian.

Kat and Phil exit the room and close the door.

I look at Kat, Phil, and Brian and ask, "What the fuck was that all about?"

Phil looks at me and says, "Jenna wants the D. She wants it bad bro."

"Shut up Phil."

Kat says, "No, Phil is right. Dr. Morris wants to get in your pants."

"Well, she ain't getting it. I'm taken."

Brian says, "Dr. Morris doesn't care if you are with someone or not. She wants what she wants, and she usually gets what she wants."

"Then I can't see her again. I won't cheat on my wife. I don't care what Dr. Morris knows about the world, I don't want to be around her again."

Brian says, "Okay. You got it. Let's get away from her office before she pulls you back in and locks the door."

I run away from Dr. Morris' door.

Phil laughs.

Kat says, "Okay guys. I have to get back to my rounds. Your truck is cleaned out and ready to go whenever you want to leave. I don't know if I'll see you before you leave. I'm heading out early to check out that mega church near the beach. I hear they are still having services once a week."

"Thank you, Kat. You have been great. I'm sure I

will see you again."

We say goodbye to Kat.

Phil and I follow Brian outside and check out the drone.

"The drone you gave me is pretty sweet. It has a lot of upgrades on it already," says Brian.

Phil says, "Cool. I have always wanted to use a drone, but the good ones are so expensive."

Brian says, "The one at your store is a great model. It has a long battery life, big motor, and can even record video with sound."

"Fire it up Brian."

Brian explains how to turn the drone on, start recording, and some basic controls.

Brian gets the drone to fly straight up and hover above us.

I look at the big display screen on the controller as Brian is flying the drone above us.

The video from the drone on the big controller is crystal clear and has good sound quality.

"There's a speaker on the controller?"

Brian replies, "Yeah, it has a speaker. You can even put in headphones to be quieter and only have the controller hear the drone audio."

Brian safely takes the drone higher in the air and above The Grove.

"The zoom on this thing is great. The drone needs to be closer for better audio recording, but the video recording can be very far away," says Brian.

Phil says, "Very cool. Now take that thing around St. Pete."

Brian controls the drone and flies it around St. Pete.

Phil and I continue to view the video on the

controller display as Brian flies the drone around.

As the drone is flying around, Phil and I see the rough sections of downtown St. Pete.

St. Pete looks to be tore up. There are overturned vehicles all over the place. Trash, debris, abandoned vehicles, dead bodies, limbs, blood, and zombies are all over the streets, sidewalks, and buildings.

"Damn. You can't even drive down these streets. So many streets are blocked off by vehicles, destroyed buildings, and dead bodies," I say to Phil as I look at the video display on the drone controller.

"St. Pete was hit very hard by the zombie apocalypse. We are lucky to have The Grove," says Brian as he drives the drone past a destroyed minivan.

BANG!

BANG!

"What's that? Where is that gunfire coming from?"

Brian replies, "I'm trying to find the source. It looks to be coming from down this street. It's pretty far away from us."

Brian puts the drone in hover and positions the video camera on the drone.

Brian moves the camera on the drone and we see a small group of people.

"This way guys! The large group of zombies was this way!" shouts a short Mexican man.

"Follow them!" shouts Phil to Brian.

Brian drives the drone around a building and stops.

"Holy crap!" I shout as I look at the video display on the drone controller.

The image on the drone controller screen is filled with a large group of zombies at the far end of the street. There must be about 50 or more zombies on the screen.

"That's too many zombies for these guys! We have to do something!" shouts Phil.

"We can't. We'd never get to them in time. It's far from here," says Brian.

Suddenly, the small group of people we are watching on the drone camera starts killing zombies.

Zombies are being shot, stabbed, hit, and blown apart.

One of the men has a unique double-sided sword. He is holding his custom double sword with a center handle grip. The man is cutting into several zombies with both ends of his long sword blades.

Another man in the group has several weapons. He has an Ash colored bamboo stick on his back, an AK-47 in his right hand, and a Glock handgun.

"That guy with the double-sided sword is really taking out some zombies!" I shout as I watch the zombies being killed.

"Watch out Felix and James!" shouts the short Mexican guy who is holding a long custom-made steel hammer with a spear tip on the end of it.

Felix looks at the Mexican guy and shouts, "Okay! Hector!"

"Fall back you idiots!" shouts Phil at the drone controller as he watches.

Phil, Brian, and I watch as more and more zombies start to make their way towards the men.

One of the men is bit on his forearm by a zombie.

Felix and James attack the zombies and clear enough space for Hector to grab the man who was bit.

Hector shouts, "Come on man! You are going to make it! We can just cut your arm off to prevent the infection from spreading!"

Felix stabs three zombies in the head and runs back to where Hector is walking with the wounded man.

James shoots several zombies with his AK-47.

DAKKA!

DAKKA!

James runs out of bullets for his AK-47 and puts his gun around his back.

James steps away from the zombies and grabs his Glock handgun.

BANG!

BANG!

James kills two approaching zombies.

James runs back to Felix and Hector.

Suddenly, two trucks come speeding down the side street.

"Who is that?" I ask as I see the two trucks.

Brian moves the drone to get a closer view.

"I can't make it out. I have to position the drone better," says Brian.

Brian moves the drone and we can see a great view of the action.

"Get behind the trucks!" shouts an unknown man to Felix, James, and Hector.

BOOM!

BANG!

DAKKKA!

Gunfire goes off from the several gunmen that are in the truck beds of the two trucks.

Hector walks past the trucks and places the wounded man onto the street.

Hector looks at Felix.

"You have to do it!" shouts Hector.

The wounded man is bleeding profusely from the

bite on his left forearm.

James holds the man's right arm.

The wounded man is fading in and out of consciousness.

Hector grabs the man's left arm.

Felix retracts one of the blades back into the center handle and leaves one blade out.

Felix asks, "Okay. You guys ready?"

James and Hector say yes.

The wounded man in a low tone of voice asks, "Ready for what?"

Felix shouts, "On Three!

James and Hector nod in agreement.

Felix slowly counts, "1, 2, 3!"

SLICE!

Felix cuts off the man's left forearm just below his elbow.

The man screams in pain.

AHHHH!

Hector shouts, "Stay with me Ken!"

Ken looks at Hector and then passes out.

"We need to get him somewhere safe," says James.

A bald white man steps out from the lead truck that is firing on the zombies.

"Shit! That's DK!" shouts Brian.

DK fires on the zombies and directs his men to keep firing on the zombies.

"There are only a couple left! Keep firing! None of them live!" shouts DK.

I look at Brian and ask, "Who's DK?"

Brian says, "He's bad news. He's part of a group called the Conquerors. Have you heard of them before?"

I look at Phil and say, "Yeah. We have heard of

them."

I step away from Brian and Phil and take a deep breath.

Brian says, "Okay guys. I'm going to bring the drone back here."

Phil says, "Sounds good. We have seen a lot. That drone is pretty cool."

Phil walks over to me.

"What's up Ry?" asks Phil.

I look at Phil and ask, "The Conquerors are here too? With some guy named DK?"

Phil says, "That doesn't matter. We have the agreement with Jacob. They won't do anything."

"I hope not, but we don't have any boundaries set for St. Pete. We will have to talk with Jacob about St. Pete boundaries now."

Brian safely brings back the drone and lands it in The Grove parking lot.

I walk over to Brian and ask, "Pretty cool stuff. Can I get a copy of that recording?"

Brian walks over to the drone and takes out a memory stick from the video camera.

"Take this. It's the memory stick with the recording on it. I have plenty of them," says Brian.

"Thank you, Brian. Very cool. I want to start using one of those drones when I get home," says Phil.

Brian says, "You are welcome. It was my pleasure."

Phil and I say goodbye to Brian.

Phil looks at me and asks, "We going home now?"

I look at Phil and say, "Yeah. Let's get home. I want to check out this video and see what we may be up against with this DK guy. Jacob may have some other tricks up his sleeve."

CHAPTER 9
WHO IS JACOB?

"What do you mean you don't know?" shouts Jacob at a woman who is sitting in a chair with ropes tied around her wrists and ankles.

The woman starts to cry and puts her head down.

Jacob grabs her hair and pulls her head back up.

"Just tell me something useful about Channelside and I'll let you go," says Jacob to the woman.

"I don't know anything. I just live there with my husband and my son," says the woman with tears in her eyes.

"Bella. Everyone knows something. I don't need much information from you," says Jacob.

Bella asks, "Why are you doing this to me? Your brother had an agreement with our Captain. Why are you breaking that?"

"My brother isn't alive anymore. That agreement died when he died. I'm trying to figure out a new arrangement between our groups. I don't want to hurt you or your people, but your Captain has left me with no choice," says Jacob.

KNOCK! KNOCK!

Jacob looks at the closed door and shouts, "Yeah! What is it?"

A man shouts, "They are back from their trip!"

"I'll be right out!" shouts Jacob.

Jacob looks at Bella and says, "Look. I'm not trying to hurt anyone else, but your Captain isn't helping matters between our groups."

Bella starts to cry.

Jacob walks towards the door and exits the room.

Jacob closes the door, walks down a hallway, and into a bathroom.

Jacob washes his hands in the sink of a nice clean bathroom.

There is some noise coming from another part of the house.

Jacob exits the bathroom and walks down the hall towards the noise.

Jacob enters the room and sees people talking in a kitchen and the adjoining living room.

There are three men in the kitchen and four men sitting in the living room.

The men look at Jacob and stop talking.

An awkward silence fills the kitchen and living room.

Jacob looks at the men and asks, "Where is he?"

A man says, "Outside."

"Go get him," says Jacob.

A man exits the kitchen and walks out the front door.

Jacob opens the refrigerator and opens a bottle of beer.

Jacob takes a sip of beer and his men aren't sure what to do.

Jacob looks at his men and asks, "What's going on everybody? Why is everyone so quiet?"

The front door opens, and two men walk into the house.

A bald white man walks into the kitchen.

Jacob looks at the man and shouts, "Hey Lane! What's going on?"

The bald man looks at Jacob with a look of irritation.

The bald man looks at Jacob and says, "I don't know why you can't call me DK."

Jacob replies, "Sorry. That's right. My mistake."

Jacob takes a sip from his beer bottle.

"Well, DK? How was your trip around Tampa Bay? Anything to report?" asks Jacob.

DK replies, "It's getting worse in both counties. St. Pete is by far the worst spot and is still badly overrun by the dead."

Jacob asks, "What about the wall around part of downtown Tampa?"

DK says, "Still no luck with finding a way inside the wall. My men took some fire around the wall, but everyone is fine. I'm going to be heading back into the Gulf of Mexico and checking in with my Navy contacts."

"Good. Keep me informed. I want to know what the military is doing next," says Jacob.

A woman's cry for help is heard down the hall from the kitchen.

HELP!

Jacob looks at a man standing in the kitchen and says, "Go shut her up."

DK looks at Jacob and asks, "Who is that? Did you take another person from another community?"

Jacob shouts, "Everyone out! Leave me and my brother-in-law for a minute!"

Jacob's men exit the living room and kitchen, and then exit the house through the front door.

Jacob looks to see if everyone is out of the house.

Everyone is gone from the living room and kitchen besides DK and Jacob.

"Do you have a problem with what I'm doing DK?" asks Jacob.

DK looks directly at Jacob and asks, "You want me to be honest?"

Jacob says, "Always."

"Well, I hate some of the things you do. I worry about my sister and nephew. I have seen some crazy stuff around Tampa Bay. I just want my family to be safe," says DK.

Jacob walks over to DK and asks, "What about me? Do you worry about me?"

DK hesitates to answer.

Jacob says, "I'm your family also. You are my brother. My only brother now."

"I'm sorry about Joseph. I can't believe he is gone. He couldn't leave that group alone huh?" asks DK.

Jacob walks towards the refrigerator and grabs a bottle of beer out of the refrigerator.

DK asks, "What's the plan for that group who killed Joseph?"

Jacob opens the bottle of beer and slides it to DK.

"They will get what's coming to them. We have an agreement of peace for now. We will honor the agreement, but I plan to get even with Ryan and William," says Jacob.

DK says, "Sounds like a plan. Keep me posted of the plan going forward."

Jacob says, "I definitely will. How was St. Pete?"

DK says, "St. Pete is a place to avoid if we can. We will need more firepower to clear out the dead and take over that area. I was only able to take over a couple of buildings, but our connection with The Grove and Dr. Morris is strong. She is on our side still."

"Good. Good. We will continue to send in groups to downtown St. Pete to take over more buildings and businesses. I know the St. Pete airport and docks are somewhat secured by the Coast Guard still," says Jacob.

Jacob finishes his beer and puts his bottle in a trash can.

DK says, "I'm going to see Beth and Brandon before I leave. I was going to head over there next after I talked with you."

Jacob smiles and says, "I'll go over there with ya."

DK and Jacob exit the kitchen and exit the house through the front door.

DK walks out the front door and Jacob follows behind him.

Jacob shouts, "The house is all yours guys! Don't drink all the beer!"

The men laugh and go back into the house.

DK and Jacob walk down the middle of a road.

The road is clean and empty.

"How's the neighborhood been holding up?" asks DK to Jacob.

Jacob looks down the street and says, "Pretty good. The front gates are holding up and we control every house in this neighborhood."

Jacob and his men have taken control of a large neighborhood in Clearwater, Florida right next to Clearwater Beach.

Jacob and his Conquerors control a lot of neighborhoods, buildings, businesses, and other properties around Tampa Bay.

DK and Jacob walk to the front door of a very large

beige house with a paver driveway and three garage doors.

"Home sweet home," says Jacob as he enters the house through the front door.

DK enters the house behind Jacob.

Jacob and DK enter the house and walk into the kitchen.

A woman and boy, who are standing at the kitchen sink, turn and look at Jacob and DK.

"Hey dad. Hey uncle DK," says the boy.

Jacob walks over to his wife and son.

DK says, "Hey Brandon. Hey Beth."

Beth kisses Jacob.

Jacob rubs the top of Brandon's head and short hair.

Beth turns towards DK and asks, "Hey Lane. How are ya?"

Brandon says, "He doesn't go by that. He's DK."

"Sorry. I forgot," says Beth to Brandon.

DK says, "I'm good. Just wanted to say hello. I haven't seen you two in a while now."

Beth finishes cleaning the plate Brandon used for lunch.

Brandon cleans his hands and runs over to DK.

Brandon punches DK in the stomach and DK falls to the ground.

"Man, you are getting too strong big guy. Take it easy on me," jokes DK.

Brandon jumps on top of DK and pins him.

"One, Two, Three!" shouts Brandon.

"You won. Buddy boy," says DK.

DK picks Brandon up from the floor and they both stand up.

"How old are you now?" asks DK.

Brandon says, "I'm eleven."

"Pretty soon you'll start driving. Look out now," jokes DK.

Beth says, "Brandon, go upstairs and read for a little bit. I'll be up in a little bit to read with you."

Brandon asks, "Can I hang out with DK for a little longer?"

Jacob shouts, "Go upstairs Brandon! Your mother will be up in a little bit!"

Brandon gets scared and runs upstairs to his bedroom on the second floor of the house.

"You didn't have to yell at him. He's been through a lot lately," says Beth.

Jacob turns towards Beth and gives her a glaring stare.

"He needs to listen better! He's getting soft!" shouts Jacob at Beth.

DK doesn't like the way Jacob is talking to Beth and Brandon.

"So, what's going on Beth? How are you and Brandon doing?" asks DK to try to change the subject and calm the situation down.

Jacob is staring at Beth.

Beth walks away from Jacob and over to DK.

"I'm doing okay. How are you?" asks Beth.

Jacob says, "I'm going to check on Brandon."

"Good idea, Jacob," says DK.

Jacob walks past Beth and goes upstairs.

Beth looks up at the ceiling and waits for Jacob to go to the second floor.

DK asks, "Is everything okay Beth?"

Beth puts her finger in the air and listens for Jacob to fully go up the stairs.

Beth whispers, "I don't want Jacob to hear us

talking."

DK whispers, "What's going on? Are you and Brandon safe?"

Beth walks into the living room.

The living room is away from the kitchen and stairs.

Beth sits down, and DK sits next to her.

Beth looks at DK and says, "Jacob has been very aggressive and mean since his brother died. He's been cold and distant since he took over sole power of our group."

"Has he hit you or Brandon?" asks DK.

Beth starts to cry.

DK gets pissed at the sight of his sister having tears in her eyes and the thought of Jacob hurting her or Brandon.

"No. Jacob hasn't hit me or Brandon," says Beth.

DK sees that Beth hesitates to respond and he suspects that Beth is lying to him to protect Jacob.

DK is a very capable fighter and soldier. He has prior military training and has a lot of connections with the military around Tampa Bay.

Jacob enters Brandon's room.

"Hey bud. Can I come in?" asks Jacob.

Brandon puts his book down and says, "Okay."

"What are you reading?" asks Jacob.

Brandon replies, "I forgot what it's called. It's about wizards and magic."

"That's cool," says Jacob as he sits on Brandon's bed.

Jacob looks around Brandon's room.

Brandon's room is very big. Almost too big for an eleven-year-old kid.

Brandon has tons of sports posters, memorabilia, toys, books, games, and art supplies.

"I'm sorry I yelled at you before son. I have been dealing with a lot since your Uncle Joseph left us," says Jacob.

Brandon looks down and gets sad.

"Your Uncle Joseph loved you very much and so do I. We all do," says Jacob.

Brandon looks up at Jacob and asks, "Why did he have to die?"

Jacob doesn't know how to answer that question.

Jacob thinks of something to say to Brandon about Joseph dying.

"It was his time. It was his time to leave us," says Jacob.

Brandon says, "I miss him so much."

"I miss him too. I won't let anything happen to you though Brandon. I will protect you and your mom," says Jacob.

Brandon hugs Jacob.

Jacob looks down at the floor next to Brandon's bed and sees a toy machine gun.

Jacob looks at Brandon and asks, "You like guns Brandon?"

Brandon says, "Yeah. I haven't fired a real one though."

Jacob says, "I'll show you how to use a gun. You'll have to learn to protect yourself son."

"Awesome. Can we go shoot now?" asks Brandon.

Jacob smiles and says, "Later. You have to read, and your mom will be up in a second."

"Can I interrupt guys?" asks Beth as she stands outside of Brandon's bedroom doorway.

Brandon and Jacob turn and look at Beth.

Brandon shouts, "Dad is going to teach me how to

shoot a gun!"

Beth gives Jacob a look of uneasiness.

"Only if your mom says it's okay buddy," says Jacob.

"Can he mom?" asks Brandon.

Beth says, "We will talk about it later. You read your book now. I will go over it with you in a couple of minutes."

Jacob looks at Beth.

"Can I talk with you Jacob?" asks Beth.

"Sure," says Jacob.

Jacob looks at Brandon and says, "I'll be back later buddy. Keep reading and listen to your mom."

"Okay dad," says Brandon.

Jacob stands up from Brandon's bed and exits Brandon's bedroom.

Beth grabs Brandon's bedroom door handle and says, "Keep reading honey. I'll be back in a couple of minutes."

Beth closes Brandon's bedroom door.

"Lane. I mean DK, is about to leave. Why does he want to be called DK?" asks Beth.

"I don't know. I remember him saying something about a code of his or something. Something about a Knight or something," says Jacob.

Beth says, "I don't get it, but I have to remember to call him DK."

Jacob sees that Beth is upset.

"What's wrong Beth? Everything okay? I'm sorry for yelling before. I'm just mad with work. We've had some problems in a couple of spots lately," says Jacob.

"What's going on around here? Anything you want to talk about?" asks Beth.

"Just a lot of groups not respecting me and our group now that Joseph is gone. They feel like they don't need to fear us. The groups that Joseph didn't totally annihilate are standing up against us," says Jacob.

"Well. They don't know who you are. You were behind the scenes before. Joseph was the face of the Conquerors. You need to show your authority and show them who they are dealing with now," says Beth.

"Groups have been asking who I am. Who is Jacob?" replies Jacob.

"That's what you have to show them. Show them who you are and what you are all about," says Beth.

Beth and Jacob walk down the stairs and meet with DK in the large open foyer near the front door.

"You need to make an example of a group and make people spread the word that Jacob isn't someone to mess with. Just don't be overconfident and arrogant like your brother," says Beth.

DK looks at Jacob and asks, "What's the plan? You having some problems with groups? You want me and my team to pay anyone a visit? Set an example?"

Beth says, "I'm going to be outside in the backyard for a little bit and then I'll check on Brandon. Good to see you DK."

DK hugs Beth and says, "Good to see you too. I hope to see you guys more often. I'll be back as soon as I can."

Beth says, "Don't be a stranger. We'll have to make a tradition of you coming here for dinner."

"I'd like that. I miss you and Brandon," says DK.

Beth walks into the kitchen and then to the covered back patio of the house.

"I'll walk you to your car," says Jacob to DK.

Jacob and DK exit Jacob's house.

"How did you get this house? I miss your old house before the world fell apart," says DK.

Jacob closes the front door and says, "I kind of miss that house too, but this house is awesome."

DK and Jacob walk down the street.

"When the world started to fall apart, I secured my house. I got a phone call from the government and military. They said that the world is falling apart and to take cover for several days if not a week. A week went by and the government showed up at my front door," says Jacob.

DK says, "I remember that day."

"Yeah. I'm glad they were able to keep you safe as well. Joseph and I met with the government and they gave us the greenlight to take what we wanted. They told us that we would be safe from the police and military," says Jacob.

"They gave you a free pass to take whatever you wanted in this new world," says DK.

"Basically. They gave us the greenlight to control things around Tampa Bay. They really helped us at the start of the zombie apocalypse around here. I'm not sure we would have been so successful with taking over all the building, homes, and stores around here without the help from the government," says Jacob.

DK looks at the homes around the neighborhood and asks, "You are doing quite well for yourself Jacob but when is it time to stop conquering places?"

Jacob stops walking and thinks about the question DK just asked him.

"I have seen a lot of crappy areas around Tampa Bay. People would kill to have it this good right now," says DK.

"That's what we are trying to prevent from happening. We can't lose what we have now. What we worked so hard to obtain. What Joseph died for," says Jacob.

"I won't let anyone take what you and Beth have. I want Brandon to be well taken care of. I will do everything in my power to keep my family safe," says DK.

Jacob smiles and puts his hand on DK's left shoulder.

"You are a loyal soldier DK. I'm lucky to have you. I appreciate your hard work. I have a couple things brewing around here. Your team and your services may be needed in the near future," says Jacob.

"I should be back around here in a couple of days. I'm going to check in with the Navy and see what is going on with the government orders around here. Let me know what you need done, and I'll do my best to make it happen," says DK.

"Thank you, DK. I will remember that. I may need you to set the tone of who is in charge around Tampa Bay. People won't be asking who Jacob is anymore," says Jacob.

CHAPTER 10
WHERE'S MY BOY?

"Thanks guys! Glad we could help you guys!" shouts TJ to Bo and Barrett as TJ and Janet walk to TJ's jeep.

Bo says, "Thank you. I appreciate it. Barrett and I will have you two over for a nice dinner in the future."

Barrett says, "Nice to meet you both. We will see you later."

Barrett drives his truck away from TJ's jeep and exits MacDill.

Janet puts her belongings in TJ's jeep and looks at TJ.

TJ walks over to his jeep's trunk and next to Janet. "You ready to get home?" asks TJ.

"You aren't going to see your father first?" asks Janet.

TJ sees a man walking towards TJ's jeep.

The man shouts, "You guys okay?"

Janet looks at the man and sees that it's Ramano.

Janet looks at Ramano and asks, "You okay? Is the chopper okay?"

Ramano says, "Yeah. I'm okay, and we can repair my baby. She will be alright."

TJ asks, "I'm glad you are okay Ramano. Did you figure out who was shooting at us?"

Ramano replies, "I couldn't see anyone closely as

we were so high up, but I could see a couple of groups of people together firing at us."

Janet says, "I'm glad you are safe and made it back okay."

"Me too. I almost didn't. The shooters were trying to hit the gas tank and rotors. In the past, the gunmen around the zoo have targeted the fuselage," says Ramano.

TJ says, "I'm glad you are safe and made it back okay. We have to get going. I need to get my boy Odin."

Ramano grabs his radio and says, "They are here."

TJ looks at Ramano and asks, "Again with this? How long do I have?"

Before Ramano can answer, a car comes speeding over to TJ's jeep.

Janet sees the car and says, "Not very long."

Ramano says, "I'm sorry guys. Again. Your dad is my boss and I have to do what he says."

"There's my boy!" shouts Rich as he gets out of his blue sedan.

"Hey dad," says TJ.

Rich says, "Hey Janet. Thank you Ramano."

Ramano says, "I'm sorry TJ, but your father wanted to make sure he saw you when you got back here."

TJ replies, "I understand. Thank you for the helicopter ride Ramano. We'll be in touch if we need your services again."

Ramano replies, "You are welcome. I'll see you guys later. Bye Janet."

TJ, Janet, and Rich say goodbye to Ramano.

"You make out okay at the zoo? Where is Armstrong, Brimley, and Roberts?" asks Rich.

"They are dead. We made out okay, but the zoo and inside the wall is a mess. We barely escaped ourselves," says TJ.

Rich looks at Janet and asks, "Is that true Janet? What happened?"

Janet says, "Yeah, it's true. Armstrong, Brimley, and Roberts didn't make it out alive. They sacrificed themselves in order for us to escape."

TJ hands Rich the name badges of Armstrong, Brimley, and Roberts.

"Wow. You aren't joking," says Rich.

"It was rough in there. Your soldiers got bit by a group of zombies. They wanted me to give you their badges to show you that they didn't make it. They fought to the very end, but they didn't make it out alive," says TJ.

"Why is your face all bruised and swollen TJ?" asks Rich.

"Roberts and I had a disagreement," says TJ.

"I thought you would have a problem with Armstrong, but Roberts is a hothead," says Rich.

"You got that right," says Janet.

Rich says, "Let's get some ice on your face. I have some medication for the swelling as well."

TJ replies, "I'm fine. It's just soft tissue damage. We have to get back."

Rich says, "You need to come to my office. I'll get some ice for your face and I need to tell you both some big news."

"What's up? Just tell me here," says TJ.

"I can't. It's classified information that I can't just tell anyone. Get in my car. I'll take you to my office and then back to your jeep later," says Rich.

Janet says, "Okay, but we really do have to be getting back home."

"It will only take about 20 minutes," says Rich.

TJ, Janet, and Rich get into Rich's sedan.

Rich drives across the base and to his office.

"Take a seat and relax you two. I'll be right back with some ice and waters for you," says Rich.

Rich leaves his office, while TJ and Janet sit in the two seats in front of Rich's desk.

"Your face looks a little better, but it's still swollen and bruised," says Janet.

"Yeah, it's okay. It will be okay. It'll just take some time for the swelling to go away," says TJ.

"I hope my boy O is okay and they didn't over feed him," says TJ.

Janet replies, "O will be fine. Odin can definitely eat, but we'll have to watch his diet when we get him back."

Rich comes back in his office with two bottles of water and a bag of ice.

TJ and Janet thank Rich for the waters and ice bag.

TJ puts the bag of ice on his left eye and cheek.

Janet takes a sip of water.

Rich closes his office door and sits in his office desk chair.

"Did you find who you were looking for at the zoo?" asks Rich.

"Yeah. We found Barrett, Bo's brother. There were a couple of survivors in there but more zombies than anything else," says TJ.

Rich says, "I'm sorry to hear that. I know people have been interested in what was going on in there for a while now."

"I wouldn't mess with that place, and I don't plan on going back in there again," says TJ.

Rich asks, "Good to know, but what are your plans?

What is next for you and Janet?"

Janet looks at TJ.

Before TJ or Janet can answer, Rich says, "I have some news about your sister."

"You have had contact with Alice?" asks TJ.

Rich says, "No contact with her, but I heard that her school was closed for some time now. A big group of military and government officials were in Tallahassee and the Northern part of Florida. A team searched her apartment. Her apartment was empty, besides some clothes and a few little things, and her car was gone."

"She might be alive. She is tough and smart, but I'm not sure how well she can do alone," says TJ.

Janet looks at TJ and asks, "What do you want to do? You want to go look for her?"

Rich says, "Alice is smart, but she might be alone. I would send a team out for her, but I don't have anyone available for the job."

"I will go looking for her. I will take I-75 North and try my luck with finding her," says TJ.

Janet asks, "Where would she have gone? Would she try to come down here on I-75 or stay on I-10 towards Jacksonville?"

Rich says, "I think she would try to come here. I think she would have stayed on I-75 to come here to find us in Tampa."

"Then we go up I-75 towards Tallahassee," says Janet.

"Great. I also want to tell you some more news about the government and military," says Rich.

Rich looks at his notes that he wrote down on a piece of paper.

"The people above me told me some interesting

information. Tampa could be getting hit with a tropical storm or even a hurricane in the near future. The radar the government has is showing a big tropical storm headed towards the West Coast of Florida. We could start feeling the effects of the storm in two or three days from now," says Rich.

"We have to warn everyone! Can the soldiers go around and let people know a storm is coming?" asks Janet.

Rich says, "We are trying to send a group of troops around different areas of Tampa Bay to spread the word, but we are running out of time and we can't reach everywhere."

"We will tell our people and spread the word the best that we can," says TJ.

TJ stands up from his chair.

Rich says, "That's not all son. Please sit down."

TJ looks at Rich but keeps standing.

"The government is sending more troops, vehicles, and people this way. They are in various parts of Florida, but I'm not sure when they will be here in Tampa Bay and at MacDill," says Rich.

"Where are they now? What are their orders? Are we in danger?" asks TJ.

Rich looks at his notes on his desk and says, "The government is still away from here. Most of them anyway. We have the Coast Guard in St. Pete and Clearwater. There is a small carrier in the Gulf that may be moving away from us depending on the direction of the storm. There aren't any specific orders just yet from the higher ups, but I'm sure they are coming."

"Are we in danger?" asks Janet.

"No danger just yet, but the military and

decontamination groups will be coming to Tampa Bay. The latest location of the deployed units was in Tallahassee, Jacksonville, Miami, Key West, and Fort Lauderdale," says Rich.

TJ looks at Janet and says, "My sister was at school in Tallahassee. She could be in danger."

"That's why I'm telling you about this son. I was hoping that you could go check it out or at least try. I know how close you were with Alice," says Rich.

TJ says, "Well, let's get going then. Time is wasting with this conversation."

Rich says, "Hold on a minute. I want you to go check on your sister, but I want you safe and the trip done right. Let me get you some supplies for your trip."

Janet says, "That would be great. We will need a lot of gas for the trip to Tallahassee from here."

Rich stands up and says, "Oh, and one more thing."

TJ and Janet look at Rich.

"I know the zoo is safe and there is a group of people living in there," says Rich.

TJ nervously looks at Rich but doesn't know what to say.

"But don't worry. I won't send in a team to go take over the place or anything. I can get around that now, since I sent in Armstrong and his men. Shame they didn't make it out. I will report that they were K.I.A. and the zoo is unsafe for our troops," says Rich.

TJ smiles and says, "Thank you. They're good people in the zoo and they want to be left alone."

Rich opens his office door and says, "But we can't have them shooting at our choppers. If they keep attacking our helicopters, then the military will want answers and will get them by attacking the zoo."

Janet says, "We will talk with them. I'm sure they were just trying to protect the zoo walls and community."

Rich says, "Let's get over to the armory and supply building."

Janet, TJ, and Rich exit Rich's office.

Rich locks his office door.

Janet, TJ, and Rich walk down the steps to the lobby of the office building.

The phone rings.

The secretary answers the satellite phone.

TJ and Janet walk out the front entrance door.

Rich is called to the front desk by the secretary.

"It's for you. It's General Godfrey," says the secretary to Rich.

"Thank you, Rebecca," says Rich.

Rich answers the phone and talks with the General.

TJ sees that Rich is on the phone.

"I wonder who my father is talking with," says TJ.

Janet says, "I'm not sure, but it looks like your father isn't saying much."

"I understand sir. I will call you back with my satellite phone. I know it's important. I'm just finishing an important meeting right now. I will call you back in 20 minutes," says Rich.

Rich hands Rebecca the phone and says, "Hold all my calls until I get back. I will be back in about 20 minutes."

Rebecca replies, "Yes sir. Captain Bailey."

Rich exits the building and walks over to his sedan.

TJ, Janet, and Rich get into Rich's car.

Rich drives to the armory and supply building.

"This place is getting a lot busier. Every time we come back here. I see knew people and more vehicles," says Janet.

"As the world continues to fall apart. More people are looking for a safe zone. The streets of Tampa are not safe by any means, but it looks to be safer than other cities and states, like New York, Atlanta, Richmond, D.C., and Philadelphia," says Rich as he parks his car.

TJ asks, "How is the rest of the U.S. doing?"

Rich, Janet, and TJ exit Rich's car.

"It's not looking good son. The major cities have fallen. Smaller cities with smaller populations are still fighting, but most big cities are overrun and are being reset," says Rich.

"Reset? What does that mean?" asks Janet.

Rich walks into the armory.

Janet looks at TJ and asks, "What does reset mean?"

Rich stands in the entrance of the huge armory.

The armory doors close behind TJ and Janet as they enter the building.

"What does reset mean?" asks TJ.

Rich says, "It's not good. If a city is placed under the Reset protocol, the city is cleared out. They try to keep as much structure, buildings, power grids, and property as they can but most of the buildings will be destroyed by the EMPs, bombs, and charges being set off."

"How do we stop that from happening here?" asks TJ.

Rich says, "I'm not sure that we can if the order is given, but we can hopefully prevent the order from being put through. If we keep the Tampa Bay area from being a total loss, then we can prevent it from being blown up and reset."

Janet looks at TJ and says, "I don't like that at all. We can't let Tampa Bay fall."

Rich says, "We aren't there yet. We will know more when the government officials come to Tampa Bay to evaluate the city and what they decide."

TJ says, "We need to get going then. I need to find Alice and get back here."

Rich says, "I will do my best to stall any orders like project Reset to Tampa Bay, but I can only do so much. If the people above me order to blow this place up, then there isn't much I can do."

"Okay. Enough of this terrible news. Let's get these supplies so Janet and I can get moving," says TJ.

Rich points to a large tank in the back of the armory and says, "That tank is full of gasoline. Grab too large gas cans and fill them up. I'll grab a couple of things for you guys."

Janet and TJ walk to the very back of the armory and to the large gasoline container.

TJ sees two large empty gas cans and grabs them.

TJ gives a gas can to Janet and Janet starts filling the can with gasoline.

Janet looks at TJ and says, "That's pretty scary that the government can just blow up a city without any hesitation. What gives them the right to make the decision that a city is lost and should just be destroyed?"

Janet finishes filling the gas can and turns off the valve that is releasing the gasoline from the tank.

TJ takes the full gas can and gives Janet the empty one.

Janet starts to fill the empty gas can.

TJ says, "I don't know, but I'm glad we know that information. If it's time to leave, then we will get the hell out of here. My father doesn't want to see Tampa Bay blown up. I know that, and I doubt the government would blew up this functioning Air Force base."

"Good point. The government needs a base of operations and MacDill is in good shape. They could still blow up parts of Tampa Bay without hesitation," says Janet.

"Let's not think about that for now. We will be informed by my father if anything is happening. Right now, we need to worry about the storm coming towards Tampa Bay and finding my sister," says TJ.

Janet finishes filling the last gas can and turns of the valve to the gasoline tank.

TJ puts the filled gas cans on a flatbed cart and walks over to his father.

Rich has loaded up two boxes for Janet and TJ to take with them.

Janet asks, "What do you got there?"

Rich says, "Let's go load up my car and I'll show ya."

TJ, Janet, and Rich exit the armory and supply building. They load up the items into Rich's sedan and Rich drives them over to TJ's jeep.

TJ and Rich load up the items into TJ's jeep.

"You got us some good stuff dad. We appreciate it. Thank you for the water, ready to eat meals, body armor, helmets, vests, flashlights, and long-range radios," says TJ.

Rich says, "No problem. If you need anything else from me. Let me know. Come to me first. Keep me in the loop."

TJ asks, "Do we have time to make it to Tallahassee and back before the storm, or should we wait for the storm to pass by first?"

Rich says, "I don't know. I would recommend waiting as the storm could come right on top of you as your driving along the West Coast of Florida, but I don't like waiting any longer than necessary."

"Okay. Janet and I will decide tonight on what to do. Thank you for your help. We have to get going home now. I miss my boy Odin and Janet misses her cats," says TJ.

TJ hugs Rich.

Rich says, "Stay safe out there. Your sister is smart. She would try to stay along I-75 and would either come to your house or mine if she made it home."

Janet says goodbye to Rich and gets into TJ's jeep.

Rich says goodbye to TJ and Janet.

TJ exits MacDill and starts his drive to Citrus Oaks.

TJ and Janet make it to Citrus Oaks and drive through the South entrance.

TJ sees Odin with Shaun in Shaun's front yard.

TJ drives to Shaun's house and parks his jeep.

Janet and TJ exit TJ's jeep.

"Where's my boy?" shouts TJ.

Odin barks and runs directly over to TJ.

"Hey TJ. Hey Janet," says Shaun as he waves to TJ and Janet.

TJ pets Odin.

Janet asks, "Hey O. Did you miss us?"

Odin barks and wags his tail.

Shaun walks over to TJ and Janet.

"What's going on guys? How was the trip to the zoo?" asks Shaun.

"It was good. We found Bo's brother and another group of people," says Janet.

"I see you ran into some trouble. I'd hate to see what the other guy looks like," jokes Shaun to TJ as he looks at TJ's face.

"Yeah. I had a problem with another soldier on the

133

trip. I'm okay though," says TJ.

"Glad to hear it," says Shaun.

TJ looks around and sees that my SUV is missing in my driveway.

"Is Ryan or Phil here?" asks TJ.

"No, they still aren't back from their trip to The Grove. What's up?" asks Shaun.

"I have some big news about some problems coming this way. I need to talk to everyone about the news I just heard, and we need to prepare," says TJ as he looks up into the sky.

CHAPTER 11
FREAKING TEENAGERS

"Dude! I can't believe I had to cut that guys arm off!" shouts Felix to James as James parks his car in the parking lot of Warrior High.

Felix and James get out of James' car and get their belongings from the trunk.

James asks, "You got everything out of the trunk?"

Felix checks his belongings and says, "Yeah."

James closes the trunk.

Jeremy walks over to Felix and James.

"Hey guys. What's up? How was the trip to St. Pete?" asks Jeremy.

James walks away from Felix and Jeremy.

Felix watches James walk inside the high school.

"You know, he only said like ten words to me the entire trip! We were gone for a week! Ten words!" shouts Felix to Jeremy.

Jeremy replies, "He has been through a lot. That was his first run since he came here. It will take time for him to open up after what happened to his group."

Felix says, "I know, and I feel bad for the guy. The Conquerors killed his entire family and group."

Jeremy says, "It has to be tough being the lone survivor of your entire group. I wonder if he feels survivors guilt?"

"I don't know what's going on in his head as he

barely talks to me. He did talk with Hector though," says Felix.

Jeremy sees Felix's retractable double-sided sword and grabs it.

"This thing is awesome. I feel like I could do some damage with this thing," says Jeremy as he extends both blades from the center handle.

"Careful with that thing. It has been through a lot on this trip. I need to sharpen the blades," says Felix.

Felix and Jeremy walk into the school from the parking lot.

"What's going on around here?" asks Felix.

Jeremy says, "Nothing much. We have had some trouble with the teenagers around here again. They keep tagging up the walls near the East fence."

"Who is doing it in here? Your father is just letting them do that?" asks Felix.

"No one in here dummy. My dad would cut their hands off for doing that in here. It's the group of kids outside of here. I think their leader is some punk named Dolan. He's a pain in the ass," says Jeremy.

William sees Jeremy and Felix walking towards the center of the high school property.

"Hello Felix. How are you? How was your trip?" asks William.

Felix says, "It was eventful. I am good. James and I made it safely back here."

Felix puts his heavy duffel bag down on the ground.

William asks, "What else can you tell me?"

"St. Pete is in rough shape. I was able to get some supplies from a hospital in St. Pete. We should be stocked on antibiotics and other medications for a while," says Felix.

Jeremy picks up Felix's double-sided sword and says, "Father, I would like a weapon like this. Can you have someone make me one?"

William grabs the weapon and looks at it.

"It's a fine weapon. Who made this for you Felix?" asks William.

Felix replies, "I did. It's custom. I have separate blades on each side of the handle. I can retract and extend the blades independently of each other. It comes in very handy against the dead."

William says, "Very well. I will have you make another one for Jeremy. Jeremy will help you with the build and get you the necessary supplies."

"Thank you, sir," says Felix.

"Go get some food and rest Felix. You look tired. I want to hear more about your trip and about James after you rest," says William.

Felix and Jeremy say goodbye to William as they walk towards Felix's room.

William walks around the property of the school and takes notes of what areas are doing well, what needs help, and what can be expanded on.

A man walks over to William and says, "Sir, we have a problem with the graffiti on the wall again. This is the third time the East wall has been hit. I hate to see The Haven disrespected like this."

"William says, "Show me, Reginald."

Reggie takes William to the location and William examines the green spray paint.

"I think we need to block this fence better and put barbed wire on top of the fence here. I know you don't want The Haven to feel like a prison, but people won't see the barbed wire as the fence is out of sight behind these buildings," says Reggie.

"That's part of the problem. No one can see this part of the property. Someone keeps hopping the fence and doing this," says William as he looks at the metal fence.

William looks at the green spray paint message and it reads, "Die Rice Pickers!"

William looks at Reggie and asks, "Why do you keep referring to our home as The Haven?"

"That's what people are calling it. I like the name, so I keep referring to our home as The Haven as in safe haven," says Reggie.

"I understand the reference, and I like it," says William.

"I'll start cleaning off the graffiti right now. I don't want anyone else to see this," says Reggie.

William replies, "Thank you, Reginald. I will have some people look at what to do here to stop this from happening again. We clearly have some trouble makers messing with our home."

Reggie says, "Freaking teenagers. I'm pretty sure it was that group of annoying teenagers that keep coming around the school."

Reggie grabs two spray bottles and stays spraying the wall with cleaning solution.

William leaves Reggie as he is cleaning the wall and walks to the center of the high school outdoor courtyard.

Bruce walks over to William.

"What can be done with the fence around the East buildings of the property?" asks William.

Bruce asks, "The wall that keeps getting spray painted?"

"Yeah. We need to stop people from getting over the fences. Luckily, it has only been some annoying teenagers and not someone trying to harm us. We need to correct the problem area with our fences," says William.

Bruce says, "I will get on it right away. It will be solved today."

"Thank you, Bruce," says William.

Bruce walks away from William and goes to check out the fencing.

William walks into the cafeteria and sees James sitting at a table all by himself.

There are other groups of people sitting in the cafeteria, but James decided to be alone.

William walks over to James and asks, "May I sit down?"

James quietly says, "Yes."

William sits down and looks at James.

"How are you doing James? How was your trip to St. Petersburg with Felix?" asks William.

James takes a bite from his apple.

William looks at James and waits for his response.

James says, "It was fine. We made out okay. St. Pete is not a very nice place right now. There are tons of dead ones there. We survived but were partially rescued by some bald guy and his group."

William becomes interested in what James' just said.

"What bald guy? Did you catch his name James?" asks William.

"No sir. I didn't catch his name and I haven't seen him before. He had a lot of firepower with him though. He had several men with some big guns. They took care of a large group of dead ones in St. Pete," says James.

"I'm glad you are okay. Felix said you made out well on your trip to St. Pete. You got a lot of medication and prescriptions from a hospital," says William.

"Yeah. We cleared out several medication cabinets in a hospital. I would like to go back out again and search for more things. All these people here make me uneasy," says James.

William looks at James and says, "Thank you for your hard work on the trip to St. Petersburg. Would you like to go back out with Felix again?"

James replies, "Yeah. He was okay. He knows how to handle himself and we worked well together. Hector is pretty cool also."

"Very well. You, Hector, and Felix will have another run in the near future together. If you need anything else from me James, don't hesitate to ask," says William.

James replies, "I will, thank you. Let me know when you want Felix and I to go back out again."

William stands up from the table and says, "I will James. I will but rest up and relax. You are home now."

James smiles as William walks away from the table.

Bruce and a couple of other Warriors are hard at work at securing the fencing around the East wall of The Haven.

Reggie has cleaned the green spray paint off the wall and repainted the wall.

Reggie looks at Bruce and asks, "Do you need any help Bruce?"

Bruce says, "Sure. We are placing some barbed wire on top of this fence. We could use a hand securing the last piece to the fence near the pole."

Reggie helps Bruce and the other Warriors secure the last piece of barbed wire to the top of the metal fence.

"That should do it. We now have barbed wire on top

of this fence, and I also put in motion lights and sirens if someone can get by the barbed wire. I will set the motion lights and sirens when we are all finished, so we don't accidently set them off," says Bruce.

Reggie grabs his cleaning supplies and painting materials and exits the area with the other Warriors.

Two Warriors help Reggie put away his materials.

Bruce sets the sirens and motion detectors and then exits the area.

It's getting dark and William has called a meeting for everyone to gather in the center of The Haven's outdoor courtyard.

"Thank you all for joining me tonight. I won't keep you long as I think we have some fun activities tonight. Just try to keep the noise down a little. We don't want to attract the wrong attention at night," says William as he stands on a raised platform overlooking his group of Warriors.

Bruce joins the meeting and sits down in a chair next to Li.

Li whispers to Bruce, "Where have you been?"

Bruce whispers to Li, "I was making the East fence more secure for us."

Li grabs Bruce's right hand and interlocks her fingers with Bruce's.

"I have heard people calling this place The Haven. I can't take credit for the name, but I do like it," says William.

Everyone smiles at William.

"Things are going well for us lately. We have had a little problem with some teenagers outside of here but hopefully we have some new security measures in place now along the East fence and wall," says William.

Reggie shouts, "Freaking teenagers!"

"Yes. Reginald. Freaking teenagers indeed. Luckily, they have only wanted to paint messages on our walls and nothing more. We need to keep an eye out for any more trouble areas that could be a weakness to our haven," says William.

"Tomorrow, I want to do a perimeter check of our entire home. Every square inch needs to be checked and rechecked. I want this place to be locked down and safe for us. This is our home, our haven," says William.

The meeting with William ends and people enjoy the night together. They are playing music, dancing, and just enjoying being alive in The Haven.

Night comes.

Everyone goes to bed except the guards keeping watch at the main entrance and parking lot.

There are two guards at the front entrance inside the fence and two guards walking through the parking lot.

A rock comes flying towards a parked car in The Haven parking lot.

The rock hits the car windshield.

The car windshield cracks and the car alarm horns start to make noise.

The guards run to the car and aren't sure how to shut the alarm off without the car keys.

One of the guards runs back inside to get the car keys to shut the car alarm off.

The guards at the front entrance look at the parking lot that faces West.

There is a commotion heard near the East metal fence.

"Come on. Don't be a pussy," whispers someone.

"I'm not a pussy. Shut up Dolan. There is just

something on top of this fence now," whispers another male voice.

A male teenager is trying to get over the fence where Bruce put the barbed wire on.

The car alarm is still going off in the West parking lot of The Haven.

"I can't get over the fence without cutting myself," says a male teenager to Dolan.

Dolan says, "Greg, you are up. Tanner here can't do it now because of the barbed wire."

Three other male teenagers and three female teenagers stand behind Dolan now.

Greg tries to climb the fence and he stops at the barbed wire.

Greg looks down at Dolan and says, "Tanner is right. We can't get in now this way. They put a long piece of barbed wire along the fence now."

Dolan looks at Greg and Tanner and says, "You are both useless. You either get over the fence or you both are on your own."

Greg tries to get over the fence and cuts his hand.

Tanner climbs up the fence and stops next to Greg.

Tanner looks at Greg and says, "We need Dolan's protection. We won't last a day without him and his football buddies."

Greg tries to get over the fence again but gets his pants stuck on the barbed wire.

Tanner tries to help Greg but falls onto the barbed wire.

Tanner's jacket gets stuck in the barbed wire.

Dolan looks up at Tanner and Greg and starts laughing.

Dolan smacks the shoulder of a large teenager next

to him and says, "Look at these two idiots Ox. They are too funny."

Two teenage girls laugh at Tanner and Greg as they are stuck in the barbed wire.

A lone teenage female and teenage male look at each other.

"Someone needs to help them. This isn't right. I don't like this," says the lone teenage girl to the lone teenage boy as they stand away from Dolan and his group.

The teenage boy looks at the teenage girl and asks, "What can we do, Madison?"

Madison replies, "I don't know Matthew, but I'm done with this group after this."

Dolan starts to get mad and shakes the metal fence violently.

Dolan's shaking of the fence loosens the barbed wire to Greg's pants and Tanner's jacket.

Suddenly, Tanner and Greg fall onto the ground inside the fence of The Haven.

Dolan cheers as Greg and Tanner fall onto the Warrior's property.

"Now hurry up!" shouts Dolan as he throws over the can of green spray paint.

Greg stands up from the ground and the motion lights and sirens go off.

The motion lights are bright and cast a bright light on Greg and Tanner as well as Dolan, Matthew, Madison, Ox, and the rest of the teenagers.

"Scatter!" shouts Dolan.

The teenagers outside of the fence run away from the fence and leave Greg and Tanner to fend for themselves.

Greg and Tanner are frozen in fear as the motion

light shines on them.

Several Warriors come running over to Greg and Tanner.

"Hands up!" shouts a male Warrior.

Two different Warrior soldiers grab Greg and Tanner.

The Warriors move Tanner and Greg inside to a classroom.

Greg and Tanner each sit in a chair and are terrified.

Four armed Warriors point their weapons at Greg and Tanner as they are sitting in desks.

William and Bruce enter the room.

Bruce says, "Search them for weapons."

The Warriors stand Greg and Tanner up and search them for weapons.

Tanner starts to cry.

Greg doesn't have any weapons on him.

Tanner has a small knife on him.

A Warrior gives the knife to Bruce.

"Sit down!" shouts William to Greg and Tanner.

Greg and Tanner slowly sit back down in the chairs they were sitting in before.

"Look at me! Both of you!" shouts William.

Greg looks up at William.

Tanner wipes tears away from his eyes and slowly looks up at William.

"What were you trying to do? What was the point of your actions!" shouts William.

Greg and Tanner don't say anything.

Bruce walks over to Greg and Tanner.

"When our leader asks you a question, you answer him," says Bruce.

William shouts, "Again! What were you trying to do

here?"

Greg says, "I'm sorry sir. It wasn't our idea."

Tanner doesn't say anything.

"Why do you keep messing with our property?" asks William.

Greg says, "We don't want to. It's Dolan. He keeps making us write these dumb messages on your walls."

"You can't think for yourself? You let Dolan tell you what to do?" shouts William.

"No sir. We are just trying to stay in his group. We don't have anywhere else to go. Our parents are dead," says Greg.

William is taken back by what Greg just said.

William takes a deep breath and tries to calm down.

"I'm sorry for your loss gentlemen but that gives you no right to keep vandalizing our property," says William.

"You are right sir. I apologize for that," says Greg.

William sees the cut on Greg's hand.

William walks over to Greg and grabs his hand.

Greg's hand has a cut on it from the barbed wire.

William orders one of his men to get a first aid kit and bandages for Greg's hand.

"What are your names?" asks William.

Greg replies, "I'm Greg and he is Tanner."

"Well, Gregory and Tanner. I'm going to keep you safe and feed you before I get some information out of you. You will stay here, and I will see you in the morning," says William.

The Warrior comes back into the room with the first aid kit and bandages.

"Let Lucas patch you up Gregory. Are you injured Tanner?" asks William.

Tanner quietly says, "No. I'm okay."

Lucas looks at Greg's hand and says, "You are lucky the cut wasn't any deeper or larger. You won't require stitches."

Lucas cleans Greg's wound and bandages him up.

William looks at Bruce and says, "Put them in separate rooms and make sure the rooms are empty. I will see them in a couple of hours."

Bruce grabs Greg and walks towards the door.

Before Bruce walks through the doorway with Greg, William stops him.

"Gregory, I will see you later. How you answer my questions, will decide on what I do with you and Tanner," says William.

Bruce takes Greg down the hall.

A male warrior grabs Tanner and walks him towards William.

"Tanner, sleep tight. I will see you in a couple of hours. You give me information, and I will take it easy on you," says William.

CHAPTER 12
HURRICANE SEASON

I drive into Citrus Oaks in my SUV with Lauren, Fran, and Keith.

"I still don't know why I couldn't just drive my car back here," says Keith to Fran.

Lauren looks at Keith and says, "You can't even lift your shoulder still. We will get your car another time."

Phil drives into Citrus Oaks and the guards close the South entrance gate.

I drive into my driveway and park.

Phil drives the truck he got from the Big Club and parks it in the street in front of Shaun's house.

Phil gets out of the truck and sees Shaun, Janet, Lisa, TJ, and Odin staring at him.

"What's up with the truck Phil?" asks Shaun.

"It's from the trip to The Grove. I'll take it back to the Big Club later," says Phil as he walks over to Shaun.

I see TJ is back from his trip and I walk over to Shaun's house.

Lauren goes into our house with Fran and Keith.

"No shit! When is it coming here?" asks Phil.

"What? What is coming here?"

TJ looks at me and says, "A hurricane. A hurricane or at least a bad tropical storm is coming to the West Coast of Florida."

"When?"

"I don't know exactly, but over the next two to three days. We will feel the strong winds and heavy rain over the next couple days," says TJ.

"Well that sucks. Should we board up our windows and prepare like a strong hurricane is coming right at us?"

TJ says, "I am. I'm going to board up my house like a category 5 hurricane is coming. Someone needs to tell Bo and William as well."

Shaun says, "I will go tell both of them. I know how to get to William's place, but I'm not sure about Bo's ranch."

Janet says, "I'll give Lisa the directions to Bo's ranch."

Lisa and Janet go inside Shaun's house.

"How do you know a storm is coming? You psychic or something?" asks Phil.

TJ jokes, "No, I just put on the weather channel and saw that storm guy talking about it."

"I wish it was that simple."

TJ says, "My father told me about a bad storm being picked up on their military radar."

Phil asks, "What do we have to do about this hurricane coming?"

"Go check your house, Matt's house, and Jon's house for hurricane shutters. If you don't have them, then you have to board the windows up or stay with someone who has hurricane shutters."

Phil says, "I'm on it. I'm going to check Matt's house first."

Phil runs over to Matt's house.

Shaun says, "I'm going to load up my jeep and get going. I'll see you guys later."

Shaun walks towards his garage.

I shout, "Can you also inform the Big Club and have the guards lock the store down and bring anything loose inside?"

Shaun shouts, "Will do!"

Shaun walks into his garage and then inside his house.

TJ looks at me and says, "My father also said a couple of other interesting things."

"Hopefully good news."

TJ says, "Well, my sister might still be alive. Janet and I are leaving tomorrow morning for Tallahassee. My sister Alice is a junior in college up there."

"That's great. I hope you find her."

"Thanks, my father also said that the government is in Tallahassee and Jacksonville right now. He isn't sure when they are coming here to Tampa, but they will be coming here at some point," says TJ.

"I'm sure. It's only a matter of time until the government comes around here. According to Jacob though, the government never left."

"Jacob's probably right. The government is here at MacDill, St. Pete, Clearwater, and they have a carrier in the Gulf of Mexico," says TJ.

"How was the trip to the zoo? I'm guessing a little rough?"

TJ replies, "It was pretty good. We found Bo's brother and another community. They are doing okay at the zoo. I think they will need our help down the road though."

"Who is living at the zoo?"

TJ replies, "Bo's brother Barrett's fiancé Darby and her group. Barrett calls them the Pride."

"Like the lion's pride?"

"Yeah, exactly like that. There are three lions left alive, a gorilla, some chimps, and a couple of other animals at the zoo. Some of their animals got out, so keep an eye out for a cheetah or two if you are around downtown Tampa again," says TJ.

"You serious?"

"Yeah. They said some cheetah's and a couple other animals escaped from the zoo. The animals could be loose around Tampa Bay," says TJ.

"Great. Another thing to worry about."

Bobby G comes walking over to TJ and me.

"Hey guys. Everything okay?" asks Bobby G.

"Yeah. Everything is good right now, but a storm is coming. We need to secure the neighborhood. Take everything from your back patio that could fly away and put it inside. I will come by later to help you out."

Bobby G looks at me and isn't sure if I'm joking or not.

"Are you serious?" asks Bobby G.

TJ says, "Yeah Bob. A storm is coming to the West Coast of Florida. We don't know how Tampa will be affected but we need to prepare for the worst."

Bobby G says, "Okay then, I'm going to get started taking care of my house. I'll see you later."

TJ says goodbye to Bobby G.

"I'll come by your house later dad!"

Bobby G goes inside his house.

"How was your trip to The Grove?" asks TJ.

"It was interesting. The Grove is a decent place. They are trying to help people. I made some contacts with two nurses and a doctor."

Janet walks out of Shaun's house and over to TJ.

"Lisa knows how to get to Bo's ranch now," says

151

Janet.

"Very good. What's that in your hand?" asks TJ.

Janet hands TJ the bag and says, "It's a survival kit. Shaun gave it to me when he heard me telling Lisa that we were leaving for Tallahassee tomorrow."

TJ puts the survival kit in the trunk of his jeep.

Janet looks at me and says, "I think Shaun is upset that we are taking Odin with us."

"I'm sure he is. Shaun loves dogs. He grew up with a dog. I think he would love to have a dog of his own."

TJ says, "Thank you for everything Ryan. We will be back. Stay safe and take care."

I shake TJ's hand and say, "Thank you. You have been awesome with everything. Good luck with your trip and your sister. I'll see you guys later."

I say goodbye to Janet and pet Odin before they get into TJ's jeep.

TJ, Janet, and Odin get into TJ's jeep.

Lisa runs out her front door with Odin's bag of food and bowl.

"Here guys. Don't forget Odin's stuff," says Lisa.

Janet rolls her window down and takes Odin's bag of food and bowl.

TJ and Janet thank Lisa and they exit the neighborhood through the South entrance.

Shaun comes out of his garage and walks to his jeep.

"You need help bro?"

Shaun says, "I got everything I need for the trip to Bo's ranch, the Big Club, and to see William. If you can help us with my house. Like bringing stuff inside while we are gone, that would really help us."

"I will. I will have everyone help out with your house."

Shaun and Lisa get into Shaun's jeep.

I wave goodbye to Shaun and Lisa.

Shaun exits Citrus Oaks through the South entrance.

I feel a strong breeze and I see dark storm clouds in the sky.

I bring in all the items that could be blown away outside around Shaun's house. I place the hay bales next to Shaun's house.

Matt and Phil exit Matt's house and enter Matt's garage.

"I think I saw some window shutters along that wall," says Matt.

Phil walks over to the garage wall and sees several window shutters for Matt's house.

"Awesome. Those should work out great and cover all your windows," says Phil.

I check Shaun's windows at the front of his house and see that they are the same hurricane proof windows I have on my house. Shaun and I won't have to use window shutters as the windows we have will be safe against a hurricane.

Phil and Matt start bringing out the window shutters from inside Matt's garage, and I walk over to them.

I see the window shutters and say, "Glad you have these shutters. I'm going to help my dad with his house next. Don't forget about Jon's house."

Phil says, "I want to bring out these shutters and then I will check out my house and then Jon's."

I walk over to Bobby G's house.

I stop in the driveway and look up at the big oak tree in Bobby G's front yard.

The oak tree is in good shape and the branches aren't overgrown. I think the tree should be okay for the storm.

"You in here?" I ask as I enter Bobby G's house.

I walk into the house and see Bobby G outside on his back patio.

Bobby G is trying to move a heavy potted plant but it's too heavy for him to move alone.

"Let me help you. That thing is pretty heavy. Let's move it under the covered part back here."

Bobby G and I move the potted plant to the covered section of his back patio.

I help Bobby G move all the loose chairs, and objects inside his house.

"Thank you, son. Some of those things are heavy," says Bobby G.

"You doing okay dad?"

Bobby G replies, "I'm okay. Just been thinking about life lately. My life and the good times I had with everyone."

"I guess that's what you do when you get old? Any regrets?"

"No regrets. Some things I would have done differently, but I think life is about lessons learned and making changes from your experiences. There aren't mistakes in life, only lessons learned," says Bobby G.

"I'm glad. I think you had a good life so far. I can't speak for the parts of your life before you had me. But for the 35 years you have known me, it's been pretty great."

Bobby G smiles and says, "Yeah. That's for sure. We have had a lot of fun and good times. I think about them all the time."

"I think you are set here. You should move your SUV into the garage and stay in our fourth bedroom. My house is better prepared for a hurricane. Plus, Lauren's parents are here now."

"Really, when did they get here? I haven't seen Fran and Keith in years. I'll be over in a little bit. I'll move my car right now," says Bobby G.

"We brought Fran and Keith back with us from our trip to The Grove. Come by when you are finished with your house and say hello."

I say goodbye to Bobby G and walk over to my house.

I enter my house and Milo runs over to me.

"Hey belly boy. How are ya?"

Milo looks up at me and rubs against my leg.

Fran and Keith are with Lauren in the kitchen.

I grab a bottle of water out of the refrigerator.

Keith says, "Nice place you have here. Much safer and better than we had in Boca."

I ask Keith, "What did you have down there? Did you board up your house and hunker down?"

"We went between our house and Ruth and Todd's. Todd's house is only a couple streets down from ours. He already had his hurricane shutters and plywood up on his windows. Since it was getting close to hurricane season," says Keith.

Lauren laughs and says, "Hurricane season starts June first. When did he put them up?"

Fran says, "I don't know but he might have been planning for hurricane season or for the zombies. The boards and shutters did help out though."

Keith says, "Yeah, the covered windows helped with the zombies trying to get in, but they blocked the sunlight from getting in. It was so dark and hot in their house."

"I bet. South Florida is always so hot. Especially when you don't have air conditioning."

155

"We had power for a while. The power lasted about two months after the reports from the news stopped and they told us to stay inside our homes," says Keith.

"I hope Aunt Ruth and Uncle Todd are okay. They aren't in the best shape since they retired," says Lauren.

A strong breeze hits the house and moves the tree branches in my backyard.

"I need your help. TJ told me that a storm is coming here. A possible hurricane is coming towards the West Coast of Florida. We need to bring in everything from the backyard and secure everything."

"Great! We should have stayed in Boca!" shouts Keith.

"Our neighborhood and Ruth's neighborhood were lost. There were too many zombies there. We needed to leave," says Fran.

"We should be fine. Our house is safe. We have hurricane proof windows and doors. My garage door is even hurricane proof."

Lauren asks, "What should we do?"

"You three bring in anything that might blow away. Put everything close to the house under the back patio or in the garage. I'm going to put my SUV in the garage."

Lauren, Keith, and Fran go to my backyard and start bringing in everything that they can.

I exit my front door and see that Matt is placing his shutters near his windows at the front of his house.

"You do this every year for hurricanes?" asks Matt.

"Sometimes the season is slow, but we are in the bad months of hurricane season now! We will get more rain and wind over the next two months!"

"Great. I can't wait," jokes Matt.

"Where is Phil?"

"He went to check out his house and then Jon's!" shouts Matt across the street.

"I'm going to put my car in my garage! You should do the same after you get the shutters up!"

"I will!" shouts Matt.

I drive my SUV into my garage.

I exit my garage and see that we still have a lot of space to bring in any loose objects.

I walk to the side of my house and see that my garbage can is full.

Lauren walks around from the back of our house carrying a patio chair.

"That garbage can stinks. We really need to dump it somewhere," says Lauren.

"Yeah. I will after the storm passes. I need to put the can inside the garage. I'm going to wait until the last minute because it smells so bad."

Lauren puts the patio chair in the garage.

"How we looking in the back patio?"

Lauren replies, "Good. Just have three chairs left and the table. I'm going to wait to bring in the potted plants and vegetables."

"Okay good. I'm going to walk around the neighborhood and check things out."

"Okay sweetie. I'll be here or over at Nicole's house," says Lauren.

I kiss Lauren goodbye and then walk towards the South entrance.

I make it to the South entrance and talk with the guards.

The wind is starting to pick up now.

"We have a storm coming this way guys. A hurricane. We need to secure the gates, lookout platform, and everything around the neighborhood."

"We should put the lookout platform down on its side towards the wall to prevent it from being knocked down by the wind," says Brody.

"Good idea. Do what you can here. You have some time until we need to put the platform down. You should do that last."

I walk around the South entrance and the nearby homes. I talk with everyone and explain the situation to them. The people of Citrus Oaks prepare for the storm and bring everything that could fly away inside their homes.

I see Carlos' house and decide to tell them about the storm.

As I stand at Carlos' front door, I feel uneasy about talking with Carlos and Gloria.

I knock on the front door.

KNOCK! KNOCK!

I take a deep breath and try to calm my nerves.

No one comes to the door.

I knock on the front door again.

KNOCK! KNOCK!

I wait a couple of seconds and try to listen for any movement inside.

I don't hear any sounds of movement inside.

I grab the door knob and try to open the door.

The door opens.

I slightly open the front door and shout, "Carlos? Gloria?"

No answer.

I walk away from the front door and look at Carlos' driveway.

The driveway is empty.

I walk into Carlos' house. I fear that they may have

killed themselves.

"Hello? Is anyone here?"

I search the entire house, backyard, and garage.

No one is at Carlos' house and the garage is empty.

I walk over to Brody at the South entrance and ask, "Has Carlos and Gloria been around? Did they leave?"

Brody replies, "I haven't seen them since they left yesterday. I think you were gone when they left."

"Thanks Brody. Let me know if they come back."

"Will do boss," says Brody.

I walk away from the South entrance and make my way towards my house.

Phil comes walking out of Matt's garage.

I'm partially in shock that Carlos and Gloria are gone and partially relieved that I don't have to worry about Gloria anymore.

"You okay Ry?" asks Phil as he sees me walking towards my house.

"Yeah. I'm good. How are you?"

"Pretty good. My house is not good for a storm, but Jon's is good. They have hurricane windows and doors. I'm going to stay there with them," says Phil.

I walk over to Phil and Matt and help them with putting up the shutters on Matt's house.

Hours go by and it becomes night.

The winds continue to pick up and it's raining.

Bobby G is in my living room talking with Fran and Keith.

Lauren and I are in our kitchen.

Phil is with Jon and Kelly in Jon's house.

Matt is with Kylie, Ann, Nicole, Mason, and Mia.

Shaun pulls up to the South entrance.

Shaun honks his horn for someone to open the gate.

Shaun looks at Lisa and says, "I hope they all didn't go inside their homes yet."

Shaun honks his jeep horn again.

No one opens the South entrance gate.

Lisa asks, "What do we do if no one lets us in?"

Shaun says, "Someone will. If not, I will hop the wall and open the gate myself."

Lisa looks back at a car that is behind Shaun's jeep.

Suddenly, the South entrance gate opens.

Shaun drives through the South entrance and the car behind Shaun follows him.

Brody closes the South entrance gate and locks it.

"That's it. Everyone is back now. Let's go home," says Brody to another guard.

Shaun pulls into his garage and the car following him parks in his driveway.

Shaun and Lisa exit from Shaun's jeep.

Four people exit from the car that parked in Shaun's driveway and they run into Shaun's garage.

The rain is coming down harder now.

"Thank you for letting us stay here. The house we were staying in wasn't safe for a storm," says Jerri-Lynn.

"You are welcome. There are three bedrooms and two bathrooms you can use. Make yourselves at home," says Lisa.

Jerri-Lynn, Kiersten, Andre, and Sam are taken inside Shaun's house by Shaun and Lisa.

Lisa closes Shaun's garage door.

The rain starts to come down harder and harder.

Several wind gusts push the tree branches around.

I look at Lauren and say, "We are in hurricane season now. I hope our weather doesn't complicate things around here."

CHAPTER 13
LET'S CLEAN UP

A few days have gone by and the hurricane is far away from Tampa Bay now.

The storm knocked down some trees and threw tons of debris and trash into our neighborhood.

I'm in my backyard cleaning up the debris that is all over the ground.

Lauren walks into our backyard through our white privacy fence gate and says, "We really need to remove the trash and debris from the streets now. The trash was building up before the hurricane blew all this extra crap into the neighborhood."

I look at Lauren and say, "Yeah, I'm going to look for a garbage truck to bring back and help us clean up the neighborhood. I know the city dump is right near I-275."

Lauren says, "Sounds good."

I finish cleaning up my backyard and take the trash I collected to the front of my house.

I add the trash that I just collected in my backyard to the big pile at the end of my driveway near the street.

Shaun and Matt have made trash piles at the end of their driveways and so have most of my neighbors.

I see Shaun add another object to his trash pile and I shout, "Yo Shaun! You busy right now?"

Shaun asks, "What's up?"

"I'm thinking about taking a trip around town to

find a garbage truck or something that will take all this trash out of here."

"Sounds good! I'm down to go! When are you leaving?" asks Shaun.

"In about 20 minutes!"

Shaun shouts, "I'll be right over!"

Shaun goes in his house.

I enter my house and wash my hands.

Lauren is petting Callie on the sofa.

Fran and Keith are sitting outside under our covered back patio talking with Bobby G.

I walk out to my back patio and see Bobby G talking with Fran and Keith.

"What's up Ry?" asks Bobby G.

"I'm heading out to find a garbage truck. The trash is really piling up around here now."

"Good idea. You want me to come with you?" asks Bobby G.

"No. You stay here. Watch over this place while I'm gone. Shaun and I will be back. I'll see you later."

Fran, Keith, and Bobby G say goodbye.

I walk into the living room and say goodbye to Callie and Lauren.

I make eye contact with Callie and say, "Bye Ya-Ya."

Callie blinks both of her eyes at me as she is being held by Lauren.

"I'll walk you out," says Lauren.

Lauren puts Callie down on the sofa.

Callie looks at Milo as Milo is sleeping on the center couch cushion of our eight-piece sectional sofa.

I walk to the front door with Lauren.

I grab my bulletproof vest and katana that are sitting

against the wall next to the front door.

Lauren hands me my thigh strap holster that has my handgun in it.

"Thank you, sweetie."

I put on my bulletproof vest and thigh strap holster.

Lauren says, "Be careful out there. Love you."

I kiss Lauren goodbye and say, "If you have time. See if you can teach Kiersten some bow and arrow skills. I know her mom Jerri-Lynn is teaching her knife skills with some blades."

"They still at Shaun's house?" asks Lauren.

"I think so. Let's ask Shaun. He's out by my SUV right now."

Lauren and I exit our house.

"You ready bro?" asks Shaun as he stands next to my SUV passenger door.

"Yeah. Is Jerri-Lynn and Kiersten still at your house?"

Shaun says, "Yeah. They are still here. I think they are in the backyard with Lisa."

Lauren says, "Great. I'll be over shortly."

"See ya later guys," says Lauren as she goes back inside our house.

Shaun gets in my SUV passenger side door.

I put my katana in the backseat and then I get into my driver seat.

"You ready?"

Shaun replies, "Yeah. I got my stuff."

I start up my SUV and exit through the South entrance.

The streets are much more dangerous since the storm hit.

Tree limbs, leaves, cars, zombies, and other random

objects are all over the streets now.

I drive down a street and see the road is clear.

"I'd say we are pretty lucky. The neighborhood didn't suffer any damage from the storm. Just some broken tree limbs," says Shaun.

"Yeah. It could have been far worse. The winds definitely blew tons of stuff into the neighborhood though. I found a car bumper, a football, a metal trash can, and a shed roof in my backyard."

Shaun laughs and says, "I had a television, a toilet, a pink bicycle, and several zombie heads and torsos in my backyard."

"I had several zombie limbs but only one zombie head. It's crazy that the zombie eyes still blink, and the mouth still opens without being attached to a body."

"I know right. Zombies are freaking weird," says Shaun.

As I drive down a road, I see two cars positioned in the middle of the road and I can't get around them.

"I think we have to push one of the cars out of the road."

Shaun and I exit my SUV and look around the area.

I grab my katana from the backseat and Shaun takes his rifle.

I step towards one of the cars and hear several zombies moaning and groaning.

Shaun looks around and doesn't see any zombies.

I hear the zombies making noises but don't see any.

I walk towards the side of the road and I see a large open canal.

"Damn. Shaun, come look at this."

Shaun walks over to my location at the canal and says, "Shit. There must be 30 zombies down there."

Along the side of the street is a canal that is used for water storage and designed to help move water away from the street and homes.

The canal is filled with dirty gross water and tons of zombies. The zombies are stuck in the dirty water and can't get out.

"Freeze! Don't you two assholes move!" shouts a man.

Two men come around the two parked cars in the middle of the road and walk towards Shaun and me.

Shaun and I look at the two men.

"We mean no harm gentlemen."

"Shut up! Put your hands up!" shouts one of the men.

The two men are dirty and look to have not showered in weeks.

"Give me your weapons!" shouts the man as he has his pistol pointed at Shaun.

The other man is holding a small knife.

I put my hands above my head.

Shaun is just staring at the man that has the pistol pointed at him.

"Lower your gun sir. We mean no harm. We will give you whatever you want."

"I said shut up! Fred go take his weapons!" shouts the man with the gun in his hand.

Fred looks at the man and asks, "You sure Lester?"

Lester looks at Fred and shouts, "Damn it Fred!"

Shaun sees that the two men aren't looking at us anymore and Shaun decides to lunge towards Lester.

Lester tries to move out of the way, but he is pushed down by Shaun.

Lester drops his pistol on the ground.

The pistol lands on the street in front of me.

Fred sees the pistol on the ground and tries to reach for it.

I kick the pistol into the canal.

Fred shouts, "Damn it! That thing wasn't even loaded!"

I point my handgun at Fred, and Fred freezes in place.

"I'm sorry mister. Truly I am," says Fred.

Shaun grabs Lester's hands and puts them behind Lester's back as Shaun has Lester face down on the street.

Lester moans in pain as Shaun forcefully pulls Lester's arms behind his back.

"Are those your cars in the road? Is that a setup to stop people?"

Fred says, "They are our cars. We put them in the road to cause a roadblock."

"Give me the keys!"

Fred says, "Lester has the keys."

Shaun searches Lester and finds a set of car keys.

"What are we going to do with these two Ry?" asks Shaun.

"I don't know. We can't just let them go."

Shaun helps Lester up from the ground.

"Does he have any weapons on him Shaun?"

Shaun says, "Lester is clean."

Fred still has his small knife in his left hand.

"Put the knife away Fred!"

Lester shouts, "Don't listen to him Fred! He's going to kill you! You have to do something!"

Fred isn't sure what to do.

Fred looks at me and then back at Lester.

Lester shouts, "Kill him Fred, before he kills you!"

Fred nods his head at Lester and then turns at me.

"Don't do it Fred! Don't come at me!"

Fred screams and runs towards me with his small knife raised at me.

Fred runs at me but trips on something in the road and starts to fall towards me.

I move out of the way as Fred is falling towards me.

Fred's momentum carries him right into the zombie filled canal.

SPLASH!

Fred falls face first into the dirty zombie water.

The zombies tear into Fred.

Fred screams as a zombie bites into his face.

AHHH!

Lester shouts, "You killed my brother!"

Lester escapes from Shaun's grip and runs towards me.

Lester trips over the same object that Fred did, and he falls into the zombie filled canal.

SPLASH!

Zombies bite into Lester's arms, and he screams in pain.

AHHHHH!

Shaun walks over to me and we both look at the zombies as they devour Fred and Lester.

"What a couple of morons!" shouts Shaun.

Shaun starts one of the cars with the keys he got from Lester and moves the car out of the road.

I look around and see that the storm did some damage to several houses. Some of the homes have holes in their roofs and large tree branches in their windows.

Shaun walks back to my SUV and says, "All clear."

I show Shaun the damage from the storm and he is

shocked.

"We were really lucky. I'm glad TJ told us about the storm."

Shaun and I get back into my SUV and I drive towards the Tampa solid waste dump.

I arrive at the solid waste dump main entrance and I see several garbage trucks inside the fence of the dump.

The main gate has some thick chain and a lock on it.

Shaun looks at the lock and says, "I have my bolt cutters in my bag."

Shaun reaches into the backseat and gets his bolt cutters from his bag."

Shaun exits my SUV and cuts the chain from the gate.

As I watch Shaun cut off the chain and lock, I hear sounds coming from the far end of the dump.

Shaun pushes open the gate and gets back in my SUV.

"You hear that?"

Shaun says, "I heard sounds of machines and people in the distance but nothing close to the garbage trucks here."

I drive into the parking lot of the city dump and see several garbage trucks.

"Any one of these should do nicely."

"Where are we going to get keys for the trucks though?" asks Shaun.

I look around the dump complex from inside my SUV and see that there is a main office building.

I point to the main office building and say, "That's probably our best bet to find some keys."

Shaun and I exit my SUV and gear up.

I hear voices and noises of machines at the far end

of the dump.

Shaun shouts, "Are people living in the dump? That's disgusting!"

"I don't want to find out. Let's get these truck keys and get out of here."

Shaun kicks open the door to the office building and we enter the office building.

The office building is empty.

Shaun and I search the entire office building and find a closed office door.

I knock on the door and hear something move inside the office.

KNOCK!

I knock on the door again and hear something slap the door.

A zombie groan is heard as I put my ear next to the closed door.

"I think it's only one zombie in there."

Shaun says, "Okay. I'll open the door. You have your gun ready."

Shaun asks, "Ready?"

I point my gun at the door and nod my head.

Shaun opens the door.

The door knocks the zombie down.

I walk towards the zombie and see that he is trapped on the ground.

I put my gun away and grab my katana.

SHICK!

I stab the zombie in his head and remove my katana from his skull.

I shake the blood off my katana and put it back in my red scabbard.

Shaun walks into the office.

I look at a picture on the wall and see several awards next to the picture.

"John Barr. Manager of the year."

Shaun finds several garbage truck keys and leaves the room.

I see bottles of water, pills, drugs, and tons of fast food wrappers all over the floor.

I look down at the zombie I just killed and say, "I'm sorry Mr. Barr. You are in a better place now."

I walk out of the office building and see Shaun enter a garbage truck.

I hear music playing and cheering coming from the back of the trash dump.

The office building is far away from the noise and music.

Shaun starts up a garbage truck and cheers.

"We got it! We got this!" shouts Shaun.

I run over to Shaun and ask, "Awesome, how much gas you got in there?"

Shaun checks the gauge on the dashboard and says, "Three quarters of a tank. We are good. I'll meet you back home."

Shaun closes the driver side door and drives out of the parking lot.

I run back to my SUV and exit the parking lot.

As I drive home from the solid waste dump, I take in the sights of the streets, trees, lawns, homes, and buildings.

I see that we need to clear out the streets again as there are a lot more zombies out now.

I catch up to Shaun who is speeding down the road in the garbage truck.

We are coming up on the street where we met Lester and Fred.

Shaun sees the car still partially blocking part of the street and decides to move it out of the way with the garbage truck.

I see Shaun speed up as he approaches the car in the road.

Shaun drives right into the car and the car flies out of the road and into a wooden fence of someone's backyard.

Shaun keeps driving and the road is clear now.

I shake my head side to side and smile.

"That guy is crazy," I say to myself.

Shaun and I make it back to the South entrance of Citrus Oaks and we drive to our homes.

I pull my SUV into my driveway and Shaun parks the garbage truck in front of his house.

Phil, Matt, Bobby G, and Jon walk over to Shaun and the garbage truck.

Shaun shouts, "Let's clean up!"

I grab my gloves and I start throwing my trash into the garbage truck.

We load the garbage truck up and Shaun controls the garbage truck to compact all the trash that we put in it.

"Let's just put the smelly gross stuff in the truck for right now and we can burn the wood and other debris later!"

The loud motor of the garbage truck is heard as Shaun crushes some trash that we put in the back of the garbage truck.

Several hours go by and we clear out all of the smelly gross trash that needed to leave our neighborhood.

Jon says, "We made several piles of stuff to burn and other trash that we don't want to burn. I don't want to burn the plastic, that may have harmful chemicals in it."

"Good thinking Jon."

Shaun asks, "I think the truck is full now. Where should we dump this thing?"

Phil jokes, "How about Jacob's front yard?"

I laugh at Phil's joke, but I don't know where to dump the trash.

Shaun says, "I'll find a place to empty this truck."

Phil says, "I'll come with you."

Shaun and Phil get into the garbage truck and exit the neighborhood.

The neighborhood looks and smells much better after we loaded up the garbage truck with the debris and trash that was piling up.

I guess services like trash pickup are valued when you don't have them anymore. I'm just glad we were able to find a garbage truck and clean up our neighborhood again.

Lauren, Jerri-Lynn, and Kiersten walk over to me.

"How's everything going you three?"

Jerri-Lynn says, "Great. Everything is great. I'm just lucky we found Shaun before the storm came. We went to our house to see how it made out after the storm blew by and the whole roof is gone."

"Really? I'm glad you weren't in it then."

"Me too. That house was only temporary anyway. It was nothing great for me, my sister, and my daughter," says Jerri-Lynn.

Kiersten says, "Thank you for letting us stay here. I don't know what we would do without this place."

"You are welcome Kiersten. You and your mom are nice people. I'm glad we can help."

Lauren says, "Kiersten and Jerri-Lynn did well with the bow and arrow training today. They even showed me how to use a knife properly."

"That's great. We have to learn all the skills that we can."

Jerri-Lynn looks at me and asks, "Do you still have your owl patch?"

"I sure do. I have it in my SUV."

Kiersten looks at Jerri-Lynn and smiles.

"I know it sounds silly, but the owl patches mean a lot to me. The owl represents so many different things and I like to think of the owl as a protector and a symbol of wisdom and knowledge," says Jerri-Lynn.

Lauren asks, "Do you have any more owl patches?"

Jerri-Lynn says, "I do not, but I'm trying to make some more for everyone."

"Where is Sam?"

Kiersten says, "She went out with Andre. They went out looking for a new home for us and some more food for us."

I look at Lauren and say, "Take Jerri-Lynn and Kiersten to the food house. Let them get whatever they want."

Kiersten smiles.

Jerri-Lynn says, "Thank you, Ryan. You are too kind."

Lauren takes Kiersten and Jerri-Lynn to one of our food storage homes in the neighborhood.

Jon comes over to me and asks, "When are you going to World of Trade again?"

"Pretty soon. Probably tomorrow or the next day. I know Shaun is trying to get back to that place."

"Great. I want to come this time. I wanted to go last time, but the whole thing with Eric happened," says Jon.

"I hope Eric is doing okay. I know that Channelside

area can flood easily. I hope they are doing okay after the storm."

"I hope so too. Let me know when you are going to World of Trade. I want to get some things for Kelly and myself," says Jon.

"I will. Plan on going tomorrow or the next day. I will come get you personally when we are leaving for World of Trade."

CHAPTER 14
TRADE MASTER

"You ready to go Jon?"

Jon says, "Yeah. Give me a second. I'm looking for my list."

Kelly laughs and says, "Jon and his lists. He probably has a list of his lists."

"How you doing Kelly?"

Kelly replies, "I'm doing well. Just a little bored. No one tells you how boring the end of the world is. I wish I had better books."

"I'll see what I can do about the book situation. I'm thinking about starting a library."

"Good idea. I'll manage the library and keep an inventory of everything we have," says Kelly.

"That would really help us out. It's important to know what we have around here and what we need to search for."

"I'll start today in the food supply houses and the medical house. I'll keep track of everything we have," says Kelly.

Jon exits from his bedroom and says, "I got my list. I'm ready to go."

Jon kisses Kelly goodbye.

I say goodbye to Kelly and exit Jon's house with Jon.

"What's on your list bro?"

Jon and I walk down the street and towards my house.

"We need some supplies. I would like to get a couple things specific for Kelly. Kelly has been pretty down lately, and I want to get her some things to help cheer her up," says Jon.

Jon and I make it to my house and my SUV.

Lauren is standing with Matt and Shaun next to my SUV.

"You ready guys?"

"Yeah. Just waiting on you two," says Matt.

I kiss Lauren and say goodbye.

Jon, Matt, and Shaun enter my SUV.

I walk to my driver side door and see Phil standing with Nicole outside of Matt's house.

I wave goodbye to Nicole and Phil.

Phil is holding Mason and Nicole is holding Mia.

Mia and Mason are getting big and are doing well.

I start up my SUV and look back at Shaun and Matt in the backseat of my SUV.

"We got our stuff to trade?"

"Yeah. I loaded up all our stuff. Even the stuff Jon gave me yesterday. You got the cards to get us in?" asks Shaun.

"Yeah. I got them in my glove box."

I reverse out of my driveway and exit Citrus Oaks through the South entrance.

"I hope that gun modification vendor is there. I brought two handguns and an assault rifle for them to modify," says Shaun to Matt.

Jon asks, "What's World of Trade like? What should I expect?"

Matt says, "You should expect a lot of people

shouting, fighting, arguing, and craziness. Picture a crazy crowded Middle Eastern market."

Jon says, "Okay, I just hope they have some good stuff there."

"They should. Last time they had a whole bunch of different stuff. I don't even think we saw half of the vendors last time."

"I wonder if we can get into level two today?" asks Matt.

I arrive outside the South entrance of World of Trade.

The South entrance at World of Trade is far less crowded this time as I drive by. Only a couple of people are trying to enter through the South entrance.

I make a left hand turn onto the East entrance street at World of Trade and I'm met by an armed guard.

"ID badge, Level two card, or other form of identification please," says the armed guard.

I hand the guard the Preferred Member East entrance cards that Jacob gave me last time we were at World of Trade.

The guard scans the barcodes on the cards and gives them back to me.

"Thank you. Have a good day," says the guard.

The East entrance gate opens, and I drive through the entrance.

I drive into the East entrance parking lot.

The parking lot is almost empty. There are only a handful of vehicles parked in spots.

Shaun looks at all the empty parking spots and says, "This can't be good. All these empty parking spots. I hope there are a lot of vendors still."

Three armed guards come over to my SUV as I park

in a parking spot.

"We need to check you out!" shouts a guard.

I look at the guys and say, "Leave your weapons in the SUV. These guards might take anything that we have on us."

The guys remove any weapons before exiting my SUV.

"How we doing my man? I ask the armed guard.

"Arms out by your sides. Spread your legs," says the guard as he looks at me.

I step away from my SUV, raises my arms to shoulder height, and put my feet shoulder width apart.

The man says, "I'm going to pat you down now. Do you have any weapons on you?"

"No sir. I don't have anything on me."

The man pats my legs, trunk, arms, and torso down and says, "He's clear. Open the trunk to your vehicle please sir."

I open the trunk and the armed guard checks our products that we want to trade.

Jon, Matt, and Shaun are patted down by different guards.

Everyone is clear, and the guards check out my SUV.

The guards check the guns, supplies, and products that we brought to World of Trade.

A guard picks up Shaun's assault rifle and says, "Nice gun. I like this model. You should get some custom modifications done to it."

Shaun looks at the guard and asks, "What do you recommend? Any vendors in particular?"

"Precision Elite Mods. They are good. My brother works there. Tell him Cage sent you. He will hook you up," says the armed guard.

Shaun says, "Thank you, Cage. I will."

The armed guards check the boxes, weapons, supplies, and products thoroughly and see that our products are safe to trade.

"Have a good day gentleman," says Cage.

"You too. Thank you, guys."

Shaun and Jon get our boxes of trade products and I close the trunk.

I look at Shaun, Matt, and Jon and ask, "No one is sneaking any weapons in, right?"

"Why, is that bad?" asks Jon.

"Yeah. This place is not the place you want to break the rules. No ammo allowed in this place. The guards have the greenlight to kill you."

Jon says, "Good to know. I'll keep quiet and a low profile in here."

Shaun, Matt, Jon, and I walk towards the outdoor vendors of level one.

As we walk towards the vendors, I see a lot less people, vendors, chaos and craziness than the last time we were here with Jacob.

Jon says, "I thought you said there were tons of people and vendors here."

Matt replies, "There was the last time we were here. Today, there's probably a quarter of what we saw last time."

As we get closer to the vendors, I see that the World of Trade took some damage from the storm and parts of the parking lot and outdoor section are flooded.

Shaun sees a gun modification vendor and walks over to them.

"Are you Precision Elite Mods?" asks Shaun.

The vendor says, "They are down a couple of tents. They have the all black canvas and tarps."

Shaun says, "Thank you."

Jon sees a vendor that interests him, and he stops to talk with the old man vendor.

Matt sees another baby vendor and stops to talk with them.

Shaun finds Precision Elite Mods and talks with them.

I see a man talking with two men. The one man is surrounded by several armed guards.

I find it odd to see so many armed guards around one man.

I'm interested in who the person is, so I walk towards the men.

The man being surrounded by several armed guards is someone of power and privilege.

As I walk closer to the group of men, I see two familiar faces.

I don't want to interrupt the men talking, so I stand quietly away from the men.

The armed men stare at me and make sure that I'm not doing anything for them to worry about.

The two men I know turn towards me.

"Ryan!" shouts one of the men.

"Hey Eric. Hey Brad. How are ya?"

Brad replies, "I'm good. How are you?"

"I'm good."

Brad directs the man that is surrounded by armed men towards me.

Brad shouts, "Abdul! This is Ryan! He's a friend of mine!"

Abdul turns towards me and puts his hand out for

me to shake.

I shake Abdul's hand and say, "Nice to meet you Abdul."

Brad says, "Abdul runs this place. He is the Trade Master."

Abdul says, "Nice to meet you Ryan. I have heard about you and what you have been able to accomplish in this new world so far. Very impressive. Keep up the good work."

I'm not sure what Abdul is referring to, but I decide to accept his kind words.

"Thank you. Your World of Trade is very impressive, Abdul."

"Thank you. We have been working hard on this place for a while. It's a constant pain in the ass. We are trying to get this place back in order after the big storm that came through," says Abdul.

Abdul looks at Eric and Brad and says, "It was great seeing you again Brad. I look forward to seeing you again. Nice to meet you Eric."

Abdul looks at me and says, "Nice to meet you Ryan. I must be going now. I have business to attend to."

Abdul and his six-armed guards leave Eric, Brad, and myself. Abdul walks towards the entrance to level two and goes inside.

Brad says, "Abdul is a good guy. He really helps me out with some hard to find meds. I don't know how The Captain would function without these pills."

"Pills? What do you mean?"

"The Captain has a drug problem. He's totally dependent on these pills. The pills are getting harder and harder to find. Abdul is my only source for them. Luckily, Abdul and The Captain go way back," says Brad.

Eric asks, "What's up Ryan? You make out okay with the storm?"

"Yeah. We made out okay. How about you?"

"We got some flooding really bad right around the docks and part of the property that is right on the water is flooded. We lost a few boats, and we had to reposition the shipping container borders," says Brad.

"I'm sorry to hear that."

Jon walks over to me and sees me talking with Eric and Brad.

Jon says hello to Brad and Eric.

Eric asks, "What you got there Jon?"

Jon says, "I got some good stuff for Kelly. I know Kelly will like what I got."

Shaun walks over to Jon and me.

"Dude, they are totally hooking me up with my gun mods. They said it will take three days to finish, but they will have them done in three days," says Shaun.

"Nice. I guess we are coming back here in three days."

"They gave me a ticket for each gun. They also gave me a free precision scope for my other assault rifle," says Shaun.

Brad asks to speak with me alone.

I agree and decide to walk with Brad.

"What's up Brad?"

Brad says, "I have been talking with Eric about things and I think we still need your help."

"I'm not sure my group and I would be a great help to you guys Brad. We aren't on the same page. The Brotherhood and Channelside aren't meshing well."

Brad says, "We aren't all bad there. Sure, our Captain is much to be desired but he's what we have. My wife Ola, Eric, Julia, DJ, DJ's wife, and tons of other people are good people. Trustworthy people."

"What are you proposing?"

"We can help each other. I will go around The Captain if necessary," says Brad.

Brad holds up the white paper bag that is holding The Captain's pills and says, "Without these pills, he's in bad shape. He needs me. I'll put in a good word with him and end the conflict between you two."

"I understand what you are doing here, but I just don't have time for people like your Captain."

"Look. We don't need him. We can have our own agreement. The Captain gets on my nerves also, but I'm his lieutenant. I can't just abandon him and the people of Channelside. There are some good people worth fighting for. Trust me, we have tons of good people you will like. We have two huge towers full of people. There has to be at least one person you'll like there."

"I don't need more people to hang out with."

I look back at Shaun, Matt, and Jon.

"I have my Brotherhood."

"Do you have fish, protein, electric vehicles, and access to a cruise ship?" asks Brad.

I shake my head and smile.

"You and that damn cruise ship. You know that's my weakness. I had my honeymoon on that cruise ship you have docked at your port."

Brad smiles and says, "I can get you a honeymoon suit on the boat. You can have a nice vacation on the boat again."

I smile at Brad.

Brad says, "We need your help with Jacob and around Channelside. If you help us with some things, I will make sure to help you out and make it worth your while."

I work out an agreement with Brad and plan to meet him at Davis Island tomorrow.

Eric and Jon are glad that I worked out an agreement with Brad.

Eric says, "I'll meet you at Davis Island around noon. I'll help you clean out the island."

Brad says, "Me too. I'll bring some people to help as well."

Brad and Eric say goodbye to Jon, Matt, and Shaun.

I check out a few vendors and make some deals.

Jon, Matt, Shaun, and I explore all of level one.

I walk over to where I talked to the old man about the RV during my first trip to World of Trade, but there is no sign of him, the RV, or motorcycle.

Matt asks, "Can we check out the doors to level two? Maybe we can get in?"

We all agree and decide to walk to the level two entrance doors.

Matt leads the way towards the indoor level two section at World of Trade.

I see the heavily guarded closed doors of level two.

A very large heavy set black male security guard dressed in military attire looks at Matt and asks for his level two pass and credentials.

I look at the large security guard and ask, "How do you get inside level two?"

The man says, "You need to know the right people to get in. You need to get a pass or badge to get in. You can get a single day pass or an all access badge."

"How do you get either of those?" asks Shaun.

The man says, "You need to be given one by the Trade Master, a council member, or another person of power around here."

Jon says, "Damn. I wonder what they got in there. It must be good if it's this well protected."

The large security guard smiles and says, "It's definitely good. Hopefully, one of these days you'll find out but it's totally worth it. Trust me."

I remember I have the East entrance pass in my pocket.

I show the man the Preferred Member East entrance access card.

The man says, "That card may get you in from time to time, but not today. Hold on to that though. It could get you in one day."

I look at the man and ask, "What's your name?"

The man says, "I can't give you my name. Just call me door man."

"Well door man, you have been very helpful. Thank you for your information. I hope to see you again and get access to level two one day."

Door man says, "Good day gentlemen and thank you for checking out World of Trade."

Jon, Matt, Shaun, and I finish up at World of Trade and start walking towards the East parking lot.

As I'm walking, I see a group of hooded figures walking towards me.

I try to step out of the way to let them pass, but they change their direction to walk into me.

One of the hooded figures gets right up in my face.

I see that the person is wearing a black mask with a white skull outline on it over the bottom part of their face, black sunglasses, and a black hood.

The person whispers to me, "I know who you are. You are special in this world. Isiah will protect you."

185

I'm taken back by the message but don't feel threatened as I look at the hooded figure.

Shaun, Jon, and Matt turn back towards me and see the group of hooded figures around me.

Shaun becomes concerned for my safety.

"What the fuck are you doing?" shouts Shaun.

The person in the black hood and mask whispers, "Isiah will protect you. Be wary of the brother."

Shaun, Jon, and Matt run towards me.

The hooded figures scatter and vanish into the crowd of people near the vendors at World of Trade.

"You okay bro? What the hell was that?" asks Shaun.

Shaun looks into the crowd of people and vendors, but the hooded figures are gone.

"I think they were warning me. They didn't hurt me. They were delivering a message."

"What message?" asks Jon.

"Something about someone named Isiah and to be wary of the brother."

Matt says, "Weird. Those people were freaking weird. All dressed in black and covered up with black hoods and masks."

"Yeah. They had black masks on with a skull design on the bottom part of the mask. I never saw that before."

"You okay though Ry?" asks Shaun.

"Yeah. They meant no harm to me. I wasn't threatened by them. I think they were trying to relay a message."

Shaun says, "Okay good. Let's get the hell out of here. That's enough craziness for one day."

Jon, Matt, Shaun, and I walk back to my SUV. We all put our belongings in the back of my SUV trunk.

I walk to the driver side door of my SUV and see a feather underneath the driver side windshield wiper.

I lift up the driver side windshield wiper blade and grab the feather.

I look down at the feather and examine it.

The feather is white with some light brown and dark brown going down the middle of it and coming out to the sides.

I open my driver side door and get in my SUV.

I show the guys the feather.

"That looks like an owl feather," says Jon.

I grab the owl patch from my glove box and notice the same light and dark brown coloring on it.

I smile and say, "I think you are right, Jon."

Shaun shouts, "What's with all the owl stuff?"

CHAPTER 15
DON'T WASTE THIS

"So, your leader is named Dolan?" asks William.

"Yes sir," says Tanner.

"Where can we find Dolan?" shouts Jeremy.

William is taken back by Jeremy's interruption.

"He lives in a huge house off Keene Road. We took over a bunch of homes in a gated neighborhood there," says Greg.

Jeremy goes to say something, but William says, "Thank you, Greg. What else can you guys tell me about Dolan and your group?"

Tanner starts to cry and says, "We didn't mean to spray paint your walls and damage your property. Dolan told us to do it."

Greg looks at Tanner with a look of aggravation.

"Stop crying Tanner. We are responsible for our actions," says Greg.

"Yes, you are Gregory. Why do you keep listening to what Dolan says?" asks William.

Greg replies, "Because I'm with his group. Dolan isn't the best guy, but his group keeps us safe. Without them, we would be part of the dead."

"Are there any adults where you live?" asks William.

"No. Everyone in our group lost their parents. Dolan and his fellow football players survived somehow and kept recruiting every kid that they could find. He has a pretty large group now. Dolan wants to take over your school. He says it doesn't belong to you," says Greg.

Jeremy gets pissed and exits the classroom.

William looks at Bruce, and Bruce goes after Jeremy.

"You two will stay here for now. It's much safer here at The Haven then out there," says William.

Tanner says, "Thank you."

Jeremy is walking to his room.

Bruce shouts, "Wait up Jeremy!"

Jeremy enters his room and starts grabbing his weapons and body armor chest plate.

"I know what you are planning to do, but it's not smart to go after Dolan and his group," says Bruce.

"They attacked us and disrespected this place! It's only a matter of time until they try to take this place from us!" shouts Jeremy.

Bruce sees Jeremy put his body armor chest plate on and grab a bag full of guns.

"I can't let you go Jeremy, not alone," says Bruce.

"Then come with me. I lost my mother and my home already. I'm not losing it again. I'm being proactive this time, not reactive," says Jeremy.

Bruce sees the fire in Jeremy's eyes and knows that Jeremy will go with or without help.

"Wait for me Jeremy. Let me get my things, and I will meet you in the parking lot," says Bruce.

"Okay. I will wait for you outside by my truck," says Jeremy.

Bruce leaves Jeremy's room, and Jeremy walks down the hall.

Bruce goes into the classroom where William is

talking with Greg and Tanner still.

Jeremy walks into Felix's bedroom and sees Felix reading a book.

"What's up Jeremy?" says Felix as he puts down his book.

"Are you doing anything right now?" asks Jeremy.

Felix stands up from his bed and asks, "Nope. What's up? What's going on?"

"I'm going to confront the punks that keep messing with our home," says Jeremy.

James and Ricky hear Jeremy and Felix talking.

Ricky walks over to Felix's doorway.

"I'm down. Let me get my stuff first," says Felix.

James walks over to Felix's doorway and stands behind Ricky.

Jeremy sees James and Ricky standing in the doorway and asks, "You want to come with us?"

James nods his head yes and runs back to his room.

Ricky says, "Of course bro."

James and Ricky get their weapons and gear ready.

Jeremy, Felix, Ricky, and James exit the school and go outside to the parking lot.

"Who else is coming?" asks Felix.

Jeremy puts his bag down next to his truck and says, "Bruce."

Felix looks at Jeremy with a shocked face and says, "Oh man. Bruce isn't coming. There is no way that your dad will just let Bruce and us go alone."

Suddenly, the door swings open and Bruce walks over to Jeremy, Felix, Ricky, and James.

Bruce is alone as he walks towards Jeremy.

Felix says, "I guess I was wrong. I can't believe your dad is okay with this."

Bruce walks over to Jeremy and asks, "You guys ready?"

Jeremy smiles and says, "Yes sir. We are ready."

Bruce asks, "You sure you want to do this with only us five?"

Jeremy asks, "Who else ya got?"

Bruce whistles.

Suddenly, a group of ten Warriors and William come walking towards Bruce and Jeremy.

Jeremy shakes his head and gets a look of displeasure on his face.

"What the hell Bruce?" asks Jeremy.

William shouts, "You can't do this alone! I won't allow it!"

"What else is new," says Jeremy.

William doesn't like the tone and disobedience of Jeremy.

William walks right up to Jeremy's face and shouts, "Jeremiah! You aren't doing this alone! Stop trying to prove yourself! We work together, there is nothing wrong with working as a team!"

Felix says, "Your dad is right Jeremy. It's better this way."

"Gregory and Tanner told us about Dolan and his group. Dolan has a large group. They don't have many guns, but they have a lot of people. Bruce and I have a plan on how to deal with Dolan," says William.

William and Bruce go over the plan with Jeremy, Felix, James, Ricky, and the rest of the group that will be going on this trip.

William takes a group of Warriors and Bruce takes Jeremy, James, Ricky, Felix, and another group of Warriors.

William and his group get into a truck and exit The Haven parking lot.

Bruce and his group get into another truck and they follow behind William.

Bruce is driving the truck, while Jeremy sits in the passenger seat.

"Your father is just looking out for us. Not only you, Jeremy. Your father is very smart, he has been through a lot in his life. Things he doesn't really want to talk about," says Bruce.

James and Felix are intrigued as they sit in the backseat of the truck.

Jeremy says, "I know. I heard part of the story about how my dad was part of a group back in China while my mom was pregnant. He left China for America and how it was tough to leave."

Bruce says, "You don't know the half of it Jeremy. You father made some great sacrifices for you and your mother. He could have died for what he did. You just don't leave the group he was a member of."

William pulls up to an entrance of a gated community.

Bruce stops his truck behind William's truck.

William picks up a walkie-talkie and says, "Bruce, this is the neighborhood. Dolan should be living in house number 35. I want to do a drive by first and see if anyone is up this early."

Bruce replies through the walkie-talkie, "Okay. Let's do a drive by and check things out before we just go into Dolan's house. It's still early morning. I doubt these teenagers will be up this early."

William drives through the partially opened main entrance of the neighborhood.

Bruce slowly follows behind William's truck.

The large neighborhood is made up of very expensive two-story homes.

Jeremy looks at the homes and says, "I guess these guys are living large in the zombie apocalypse."

William and Bruce slowly drive through the neighborhood and don't see anyone outside.

The streets are somewhat clear, but they have trash, debris, and tons of alcohol bottles everywhere.

William sees house number 35 on his right and stops.

House number 35 is a huge two-story mansion that is set back from the street. The property has a very secure and solid thick brick wall that surrounds it. The house has two long driveways that can hold a lot of vehicles.

William examines house number 35, the open gate, the two driveways, the property, and the brick wall.

William sees tons of sports cars and vehicles in the driveway but no one outside of the house.

William drives away from the house and Bruce follows.

Bruce and William drive down a street and turn around in a cul-de-sac.

William checks to see if anyone is around.

Bruce and William park their trucks in the cul-de-sac.

The neighborhood is safe and quiet.

William exits his truck and so does Bruce.

William and Bruce gather everyone together and decide what the next step is.

"This place is silent. Let's keep it that way. Stealth is our best option. House number 35 is where we need to go. Greg and Tanner said that Dolan lives there with most of his group," says William.

Bruce says, "William and I will lead our groups into the house. Make sure you have your weapons ready. These people could attack us. Let's stay hidden and take cover if necessary."

William says, "I saw the gate to Dolan's house is open. They probably don't have power in the house, so it could be somewhat dark inside. Be careful and quiet. We want to talk with Dolan and his people first. We do not want to kill these kids."

Jeremy looks at William.

"Let's gear up and get ready to go to Dolan's house. We will leave in five minutes," says William.

William walks over to Jeremy and says, "Jeremiah, you need to calm down. We are handling this situation. We can't just go in and kill these kids. There might be good people in the house."

Jeremy looks at William and says, "You are right father. I'm just pissed that this group disrespected our home and our people."

"Better get used to it son. Hate, disrespect, and violence isn't going away any time soon. This new world is full of it," says William.

Five minutes goes by and William gets his team together.

Bruce gets his team together and drives to the large metal gate at the front entrance of Dolan's house.

Jeremy slowly pushes open the entrance gate and runs back to Bruce's truck.

William drives through the entrance of Dolan's house.

There are sports cars and several vehicles blocking the driveway as William drives towards the house.

William needs to drive on the overgrown front yard to get to the front door of the house.

Bruce drives his truck behind William.

William and Bruce position their trucks toward the exit driveway of the house, in case they need to leave in a hurry.

William says into the walkie-talkie, "We are in position. We are going in the front. Bruce's team goes through the back. Keep quiet everyone."

William and his team exit from his truck.

Bruce, Jeremy, Ricky, Felix, James, and the rest of the Warriors exit from Bruce's truck.

Bruce and his team run around the house and to the backyard.

William walks towards the front door and sees that one of the garage doors is open.

William points to the open garage door and he leads his group into the open garage.

Bruce leads his team into the backyard and back patio.

The swimming pool is green and stinks. Without the pool pump working and no chlorine in the pool, the pool will turn green and full of algae.

Bruce opens the screen door near the pool, and he walks towards the large back patio of the house.

Jeremy holds the screen door open, and the team follows Bruce.

Bruce sees a sliding glass door is slightly open, and he walks towards it.

Bruce clicks his walkie-talkie call button one time to signal William that he's inside the house.

William hears the beep from Bruce as he is about to open a door that leads from inside the garage into the house.

William clicks his walkie-talkie call button.

Bruce hears the beep and stops.

William walks into the house through the garage and stops.

The house is quiet.

Bruce walks into the living room and sees a group of teenagers sleeping on a large sofa and the floor.

Bruce and his team walk into the kitchen.

William and his team make it to the kitchen also.

William points to the second floor.

Bruce whispers, "We will go upstairs. You cover us down here."

William nods his head yes.

Bruce, James, Ricky, Jeremy, Felix, and two other Warriors exit the kitchen and walk towards the front foyer.

There are two large staircases that lead up to the second floor.

Bruce, James, Ricky, and Felix go up one staircase, while Jeremy and two other Warriors go up the other staircase.

Bruce and Jeremy meet at the top of the staircase on the second floor.

Bruce whispers, "We need to clear these bedrooms and find Dolan."

Jeremy nods his head in agreement.

William whispers to his team, "Let's clear the downstairs. Keep quiet."

William and his team walk through the first floor and clear each room. The living room is the only room on the first floor that has people in it.

William directs two armed Warriors to keep an eye on the living room.

Bruce and Felix clear two rooms on the second floor.

James, Ricky, and two Warriors find two bedrooms full of people.

Ricky, James, and the two Warriors keep an eye on the people in the two bedrooms, but they do not wake them up.

Jeremy is walking towards the master bedroom on the second floor.

Jeremy walks towards the master bedroom and whispers to himself, "I know you are in here Dolan."

Jeremy makes it to the slightly opened master bedroom door and hears two people talking.

"I want some pancakes," says a girl.

"Well, go make yourself some pancakes," says a boy.

The boy and girl kiss as they lie in bed next to each other.

Jeremy waits by the master bedroom door and looks at his handgun in his right hand. He makes sure the safety is off and tries to stop his right hand from shaking.

Jeremy hears some movement in the master bedroom.

The boy in the master bedroom gets up out of bed and looks in the full-length mirror that sits in the corner of the bedroom.

"Man, I'm freaking sexy," says the boy as he runs his right hand through his spikey hair and then flexes his right biceps muscle.

The girl in the master bedroom bed says, "You sure are Dolan."

Jeremy hears the girl call the boy Dolan.

The girl that was talking with Dolan gets out of bed

and walks into the connected master bathroom.

Jeremy looks down the hallway and isn't sure whether he should go into the master bedroom or wait.

Dolan sits down on the edge of his bed and asks, "What do I want to take today?"

Jeremy becomes impatient and decides to go in the master bedroom alone.

Jeremy slowly pushes open Dolan's master bedroom door.

Dolan looks at the door and shouts, "Ox, that better not be you messing around again!"

Dolan stands up from his bed.

Jeremy slowly enters the master bedroom with his gun pointed at Dolan.

"Who the fuck are you?" shouts Dolan.

Jeremy shouts, "Shut the fuck up! Put your hands up!"

Dolan shouts, "You don't tell me what to do! You slanty eyed piece of shit!"

Jeremy shouts, "I should just kill you right now. The world would be better without you in it!"

"I know who you are. You are from that group that took over the school. My school. My crew and I ran that school," says Dolan.

The girl comes out from Dolan's bathroom.

The girl sees Jeremy and screams.

AHHHH!

The high-pitched scream wakes everyone up in the house and causes a bunch of shouting and screaming by Warriors and Dolan's group.

Jeremy looks at the girl and says, "Please stop screaming."

Dolan charges Jeremy.

Jeremy drops his gun.

Dolan and Jeremy are fighting now.

Bruce runs into the master bedroom and pushes Dolan off Jeremy.

Dolan falls to the floor.

Dolan sees Jeremy's gun on the floor and goes to grab it.

Bruce runs towards the gun and kicks Dolan in the face before Dolan can grab the gun.

WHAPP!

Dolan is knocked out by Bruce's kick.

Jeremy picks up his gun from the floor.

Bruce and Jeremy carry Dolan downstairs and outside.

William and the rest of the Warriors have moved all of Dolan's group outside into the backyard.

Bruce and Jeremy place Dolan on the grass in front of William.

"Anyone else inside?" asks William.

"A girl in the master bedroom," says Jeremy.

"Go get her and bring her out here. I need to talk with them all," says William.

Jeremy and Felix go get the girl from the master bedroom and bring her outside to the rest of the group.

William looks down at Dolan and asks, "Really? Superhero boxer shorts? You couldn't put something on him?"

Bruce says, "He was knocked out. I wasn't worried about dressing him."

Felix and Jeremy stand next to Bruce and James.

"I am William, and these are my Warriors. We are not going to hurt you. We only want your disrespect and vandalism to stop," says William.

"What happened to Tanner and Greg?" asks a girl.

Jeremy shouts, "We killed them!"

The teenagers gasp in fear.

William looks at Jeremy and says, "No we didn't."

Jeremy smiles.

"Gregory and Tanner are safe at our home. We welcome any of you to join us there. It's not safe out here. If you join us at The Haven, then you will be one of us. You will have food, shelter, water, and electricity."

The teenagers get excited when they hear the mention of electricity.

A girl asks, "Do you have phone service? I haven't been able to get a hold of anyone for months."

William looks at the girl and says, "We do not. The cell towers aren't working still."

Bruce says, "You will be safe with us. We will take anyone who wants to come with us."

No one moves from the backyard.

William says, "We will leave you alone now. You know where to find us and we know where to find you. Please do not vandalize our home again. We will not be so kind next time."

Dolan makes a moan as he lies face down on the grass.

William looks directly at the teenagers and says, "Don't waste this chance in this new world. We can rebuild this world, and it starts with you."

Bruce, William, and the rest of the Warriors walk towards the backyard fence to the front of the house.

Dolan gets up from the ground and runs towards a Warrior.

Dolan pushes down the Warrior and grabs the handgun that was in the Warriors' holster.

William and Bruce turn back towards Dolan.

Dolan points the handgun at William and shouts, "You! You can't just come into our home and take over! I run this! These are my people!"

William puts his hands up and says, "No son. Put the gun down. We mean no harm. We want peace actually."

Dolan points the gun at William's face.

"You don't deserve the school! We do! That was our school before the world fell apart!" shouts Dolan.

The teenagers look at each other and want someone to stop Dolan.

"Put the gun down Dolan! It's over! William and his people aren't here to hurt us!" shouts a teenage girl.

Dolan turns to face the girl who was shouting at him.

WHAPP!

A very large teenage boy punches Dolan in the face. Dolan is knocked out again.

Dolan drops the gun and lands face first in the grass.

"That a boy, Ox!" shouts a teenager.

Ox looks at a teenage girl, smiles, and says, "It's over now, Emily."

Emily smiles back at Ox and says, "Good job, Ox."

Ox picks up the handgun and hands it to William.

"I'm sorry about Dolan. We won't bother you anymore," says Ox.

William takes the handgun from Ox.

Emily looks at William and says, "Thank you, William. We won't waste this second chance."

CHAPTER 16
IT'S ELECTRIC

It's mid-morning, and I'm packing up my SUV for our trip back to Davis Island.

Bobby G walks over to me and says, "I'm coming with you. I can't say in this house and neighborhood any longer."

"Okay. Get your stuff and put it in here."

Bobby G thought I was going to put up a fight against him coming and is taken back by my acceptance of his request.

Bobby G goes back into his house to get his gear and weapons.

Phil walks over to me and asks, "How many vehicles are you trying to bring back?"

"All of them on the island."

"How many is that?" asks Phil.

"I think at least five, but it could be ten. I want all the electric vehicles. I remember seeing two electric trucks and three electric cars."

"It's Electric!" shouts Phil.

I laugh as Phil is singing the heavy metal song.

Phil grabs a stick and pretends it's a microphone.

Shaun and Matt come over to my SUV and watch Phil dancing around.

"What is going on over here?" asks Shaun.

"Phil is excited for the electric vehicles."

Matt says, "Oh, I get it. That's why he's yelling it's electric."

Phil throws the stick at Matt and hit's Matt in the leg.

"You can put some stuff in my SUV as well. I'm taking mine too. We will need to move the concrete barricades near the entrance of Davis Island to get the vehicles off the island," says Phil.

I hold up some plastic explosives and say, "I got that covered."

"Nice, but let's try to move the barricades with my SUV first. We shouldn't waste the plastic explosives. We might need them down the road," says Phil.

Kelly drives down my street and stops at the edge of my driveway.

Jon gets out of Kelly's car with his shield, a gun, and Silencer.

Shaun, Matt, Phil, and I watch as Jon kisses Kelly goodbye.

Kelly drives towards Shaun's house and turns around in the cul-de-sac.

We all wave bye to Kelly as she drives by my house and towards the back of the neighborhood.

"Mom drop ya off at the front door today? Is it the first day of school for little Jon?" jokes Matt.

Jon says, "Shut up Matt. Kelly just wanted to say goodbye to me before I left."

Jon grabs his crotch and shouts, "I'll show ya little Jon right here."

We all laugh at Jon's joke.

"Alright guys. We are all ready to go. Just waiting on Bobby G now."

"Oh shit, Bobby G is coming. Nice. Let's roll out

the red carpet. We have a celebrity coming with us," jokes Matt.

I look at Matt and say, "You got jokes today Matt. It's good to see you being the pain in the ass I know and love."

Matt and Shaun place some of their gear in Phil's SUV.

"Make sure you got everything. When Bobby G is ready, we are leaving."

Matt checks his bag and sees that he forgot something.

"I'll be right back," says Matt.

Shaun shouts, "Get your shit together bro!"

Bobby G walks out of his house and towards Phil's SUV.

I start clapping for Bobby G, and the guys start clapping as well.

Bobby G smiles and asks, "What's the applause for?"

I joke, "Because we don't have to fear, Bobby G is here."

Bobby G replies, "Always remember that. Never fear Bobby G is here."

"Sounds good Bob. Put your stuff in the SUV and let's get going."

Matt runs back to my SUV, and he is ready.

Jon, Matt, and I get into my SUV.

Phil, Shaun, and Bobby G get into Phil's SUV.

I reverse out of my driveway and see Nicole, Lauren, Kylie, and Lisa standing in Matt's driveway.

I wave goodbye to the ladies and start my drive towards Davis Island.

Phil reverses out of Bobby G's driveway, exits

Citrus Oaks, and follows behind me.

As I'm driving down the road, I see two large gas trucks at a gas station.

I slow down and look at the trucks.

Jon looks at the name on the side of the gas truck and says, "S. Willis drillers."

"I wonder what they are doing at the gas station?" asks Matt.

I stop outside of the gas station and see several large gentlemen working around the gas station pumps.

I grab my walkie-talkie and ask, "You seeing this Phil?"

Phil replies through the walkie-talkie, "Yeah. I think they are getting the gas from the tanks in the ground."

I look at the workers at the gas station and see a very large black man carrying a huge wrench over his right shoulder.

The gas trucks are very loud.

Jon rolls his window down and shouts, "Hey! What are you guys doing?"

The large black man looks at Jon and smiles.

The large black man walks over to Jon and says with a thick Southern accent, "We are drillin into the ground and gettin all the gasoline that is stuck down in the tanks."

The large black man is intimidating to look at with his oversized muscles in a small white tank top, but he sounds like a gentle soft spoken nice man with his Southern accent.

A bald white guy in a polo shirt yells at the man that Jon is talking with.

"Duncan! We need your help!" shouts the bald white guy.

"Nice talkin wit cha, but I gotta get back to work.

Have a good day. Stay safe," says Duncan, before he gets back to work.

Jon looks at me and says, "That guy looked familiar."

"I'm just glad he didn't hit my car with his huge wrench. Did you see how big that thing was?"

I continue driving down the road and make it to the entrance of Davis Island.

There are a couple of zombies near the entrance but not nearly as many as we encountered the last time we were here.

I park my SUV, and Phil parks his SUV next to mine.

Jon, Matt, and I look at downtown Tampa, at the bay, and around the streets.

The streets around downtown Tampa have taken on a lot of water. The hurricane must have flooded most of the area around downtown Tampa.

Jon walks to the back of my SUV trunk, opens the trunk, and gets Silencer.

Jon decapitates the zombies that were aimlessly walking around the entrance of Davis Island.

I get out of my SUV and feel the warm humid air.

It's a hot summer day in Tampa, Florida.

The guys, Bobby G, and I gear up and look at the concrete barricades.

There are four barricades that we need to move out of the way, so we can get the electric vehicles off the island.

"What if I push the concrete barricades with my SUV plow?" asks Phil.

"I think we have to try that first."

Jon says, "Slowly push into the barricades, Phil.

Don't try to ram into them at high speed."

Phil gets in his SUV and drives to the barricades.

Phil slowly positions his SUV plow against two concrete barricades.

"You are good!" I shout to Phil as his plow just touches the front two barricades.

Phil slowly drives into the barricades, and the concrete barricades start to slide.

Phil sees the barricades slide a little and decides to push down on his gas pedal.

The concrete barricades are sliding a little more, but they aren't pushed out of the way fully.

Phil pushes down harder on his gas pedal and his SUV rear tires start to screech.

White smoke starts to fill the air from Phil's rear SUV tires.

We all move away from the smoke.

The whole area is filled with smoke now.

I start coughing from the smoke and run down the street.

Some noise is heard from the smoke, but we can't see anything.

A vehicle door opens and then shuts.

The tire smoke clears, and Phil walks through the smoke.

"Ta-da!" shouts Phil.

Phil pushed the concrete barricades out of the way enough, so that his SUV could get into the street on Davis Island.

"Good job Phil."

I get into my SUV, as Jon, Shaun, and Bobby G get into Phil's SUV.

We drive onto Davis Island and park in front of a

million-dollar mansion that has an electric truck parked in the driveway.

Bobby G gets out of Phil's SUV and says, "Now this is living. This place is awesome."

I look at Bobby G and shout, "You thinking about getting a place here? I'm sure the homes are dirt cheap right now!"

Three men come running towards us in the middle of the street.

We all look at the men and point our guns at them.

"At ease guys! It's us!" shouts Eric.

Eric, Brad, and another man from Channelside come over to us.

"What's up Brad?"

"We heard the commotion and saw the smoke from the docks. We thought it had to be you guys," says Brad.

"Yeah, sorry about that. I see the streets are still flooded from the storm. How are your docks, the port, and walls holding up?"

Brad says, "We fixed the problem areas and we are still clearing out the water at the port and docks."

Phil, Jon, and Matt go into the house where the electric truck is parked.

Shaun and Bobby G check out another nearby house.

Eric hands me a small bag.

I look at the bag and ask, "What's this?"

Eric says, "A present."

I open the bag and see a bunch of keys. There are some vehicle keys and some house keys in the bag.

"People don't plan on coming back here. I rounded up a bunch of house and vehicle keys from the people in my building. I got three electric car keys," says Eric.

I reach into the bag and pull out several vehicle keys.

I see the emblem of the electric car manufacturer on the keys and smile.

Brad introduces me to the guy that came with him and Eric.

"Ryan, this is Carmine. Carmine and his sister Trish are people we can trust," says Brad.

"Nice to meet you Carmine."

Brad, Carmine, and Eric help us go through the homes and get the vehicles ready for transport home.

"This electric car is dead, and we can't charge it here," says Jon.

"Okay, it stays here then. Not sure how we will be able to charge this car without electricity in the house."

Phil pushes down on the gas pedal of the electric truck and shouts, "That's so weird! It makes no noise!"

Shaun and Bobby G load up my SUV with stuff they found in a couple of homes.

Brad and Eric load up their boat with some supplies they took from the homes on Davis Island.

"Where you from Carmine?"

Carmine replies, "New York. The Bronx. My sister and I came down here with my parents a couple years ago."

"That's cool. New York is a little too crazy for me."

"I miss New York and the food. I miss my parents also, they died months ago," says Carmine with his New York accent.

"I'm sorry to hear that Carmine."

"Thank you, Ryan. My parents were pretty old. I guess it was their time to go," says Carmine.

Eric and Brad come over to me and place a large

cooler in the back of the electric truck.

"What's in the cooler?"

Eric opens the lid of the cooler, and I see a bunch of fish fillets on ice.

Phil comes over to me, looks in the cooler, and says, "Nice. I miss having a high protein diet."

Shaun comes over and asks, "Is that white fish?"

Brad says, "It's a mix of different fish. Trish and I caught a lot of these ourselves."

"Thank you, Brad. The fish will really help a lot. We are getting sick of the ready to eat military meals and same old food we have been eating for months."

Shaun looks at Matt and says, "I like the military meals."

Matt says, "You would."

Brad looks at us and says, "Now that we helped you guys here and gave you some fish, we have a favor to ask."

Phil says, "I know where this is going."

"We still need your help with Jacob and his group. They have increased their kidnappings and efforts around our home," says Brad.

"Those pricks even started to come around the water now. Luckily, we can block off the port and docks still," says Carmine.

"What do you want from us?"

"We need you to talk with Jacob. Try to stop him from attacking us and trying to get inside Channelside," says Brad.

"Why don't you fight back? You have the towers and a lot of people," says Phil.

Brad replies, "We have people, but they don't want to fight. They are too lazy to fight and want someone else to do it for them."

"You want us to sacrifice ourselves?" asks Shaun.

Brad doesn't know what to say.

Eric says, "We want to keep Channelside alive and keep our connection with you going. We can't do that if Channelside is conquered."

I listen to Eric, Brad, Shaun, and Phil's points.

I look at Brad and say, "I will not sacrifice myself or my people for you or anyone. Our safety and well-being are my priority."

Brad says, "I understand."

I look at the electric vehicles, supplies, and fish that Brad, Eric, and Carmine helped us get.

"I will talk with Jacob. I want to see what his deal is with Channelside and what he is planning."

"Thank you, Ryan," says Brad.

"I promise nothing though. Jacob could still attack you. Your Captain should be the one to talk with Jacob and set up an agreement or arrangement."

Brad says, "You are right Ryan. I'm trying to get The Captain to meet with Jacob and end their attacks and kidnappings."

"And?"

"The Captain has been going through withdrawals lately. I just got him his drugs. After a couple days of the drugs getting back into his system, he should be functional again," says Brad.

I exchange handshakes with Brad, Eric, and Carmine.

The Brotherhood and I thank Eric, Carmine and Brad for everything they did for us.

Jon, Shaun, Bobby G, and Matt get into their electric vehicles.

Phil gets into his SUV.

I look at Brad and say, "We will be in touch. Davis Island is clear of zombies right now, but the concrete barricades aren't blocking the entrance road now. Remember that if you and your people come here."

Brad says, "Thank you, Ryan. I will be in touch. We can check out the huge mansions on Bayshore Boulevard next time."

"And the cruise ship?"

"And the cruise ship, Ryan," says Brad with a smile on his face.

I get into my SUV and honk my horn.

BEEP!

Jon leads our convoy out of Davis Island and back home to Citrus Oaks.

CHAPTER 17
NEW ORDERS

KNOCK! KNOCK!

"Come in," says Rich as he sits at his desk in his office.

The receptionist walks into Rich's office.

"Hey Rebecca, please sit down," says Rich.

Rebecca sits down in a chair that is positioned in front of Rich's desk.

"Sir, may I ask you something?" asks Rebecca.

"Sure, anything Rebecca," says Rich.

Rich stands up and closes his office door.

Rebecca seems nervous as she sits in the chair in front of Rich's desk.

"Sir, I'm just nervous about Tampa. I live here. My family lives here. What is the plan for Tampa Bay?" asks Rebecca.

"You know I can't tell you specifics Rebecca, but I will keep you safe and Tampa safe for as long as I can. I live here also. I don't want anything bad to happen here," says Rich.

Rebecca starts to cry.

Rich comforts Rebecca.

"What's wrong? We are safe here," says Rich.

Rebecca looks up at Rich with tears in her eyes and says, "But for how long? How long until the government decides to blow this place up? I have heard stories about other cities being blow up by our military. Something about a reset or something."

"Project Reset is not here yet. Yes, other cities have been cleared out, but they were lost in the eyes of the government. We can't have this zombie thing spreading any more than it is. Tampa Bay is not on the radar for a reset yet. There are usually other orders and projects that come before that," says Rich.

Rebecca looks to be a little relieved after Rich's comments.

"My husband and I got a puppy before the world changed. Life has just been so crazy around here for so long. I'm sorry to come to you, but I didn't know who else to come to," says Rebecca.

Rich says, "I'm here for you Rebecca. You have been a great employee for so many years now. I see you as part of my family. I have you, my son TJ, and my daughter Alice."

TJ is driving down an open highway.

The highway is clear up ahead.

TJ's jeep passes a sign that reads:

I-75 North

Odin barks as TJ passes an abandoned car on the side of the road.

"What is it boy?" asks TJ.

Odin looks out the open rear passenger side window of TJ's four door jeep.

"I'm just glad your house is safe after the storm. Every time I see a house that is damaged or an abandoned vehicle, I feel grateful for what we have," says Janet as she looks at TJ.

TJ and Janet have been driving for several hours now. They left two days later than they wanted to, due to the storm hitting Tampa Bay.

"My cats should be good for four days. Five at the most," says Janet.

TJ says, "We are almost to Gainesville now. I think we check out Gainesville first then continue up to Tallahassee if necessary. I don't plan on being away from home longer than four days."

Janet looks at TJ and asks, "You sure your sister would come towards Tampa? She wouldn't go more West into the pan handle or another state?"

TJ takes a deep breath and says, "I don't know where she would go exactly, but I think she would try to come home to see our parents and me."

"What if she was dating someone, and they lived in Alabama or something?" asks Janet.

TJ thinks about Janet's questions, and he doesn't know the answer.

TJ and his younger sister Alice haven't always had the closest relationship, but they love each other. TJ missed some years with Alice when he was in the Marines.

"I wish I knew. I wish I talked to her more than just around the holidays, when she was home from school. I just don't know," says TJ.

Janet senses TJ becoming upset.

Janet tries to keep things positive and says, "We will find her. Don't worry about that. She is your sister, so she is smart and knows how to survive."

TJ smiles and says, "Alice is pretty smart. She is smarter than me. She's going to school to be a doctor, I think. At least that was the plan the last time I talked to her about it."

TJ drives down the open highway and sees a sign. The sign reads:

Gainesville 10 MILES

TJ sees the sign and says, "I think we check Gainesville first. I'm going to get off at the next exit and we can search around."

"What kind of car does Alice have?" asks Janet.

"She has a black SUV," says TJ.

"Everyone loves their SUVs," jokes Janet.

I drive my SUV into my driveway.

Phil parks his SUV in Bobby G's driveway.

Jon and Shaun park their electric vehicles in front of Shaun's house.

Bobby G and Matt park their electric vehicles in the street next to Bobby G's house.

"Those electric cars can really move. I thought they were going to be slow as shit, but my car wasn't slow at all," says Bobby G.

Jon and Shaun unload the supplies they got from Davis Island and place the charger for the electric vehicles in Shaun's garage.

Matt says, "Ryan give me a hand. Let's get this vehicle charger out of my truck and put it in Bobby G's garage."

Bobby G says, "Let me move my SUV out of the garage."

Bobby G runs into his house and gets his SUV keys.

I help Matt get the heavy electric vehicle charger out of the truck bed.

"You really going to talk with Jacob?" asks Matt.

"Yeah, I have to. Channelside can help us."

"They are the type of people who think they are above everyone else though. They are the rich snobs that don't fly coach and think their shit don't sink," says Matt.

Phil grabs the cooler with the fish in it and takes it

into my house.

Bobby G comes out with his SUV keys and moves his SUV out of his garage.

Matt and I carry the heavy vehicle electric charger into Bobby G's garage and hook it up.

"Glad we got some solar panels for Bobby G's house. Not sure how we could power this bad boy without the solar panels," says Matt.

"Me too. We need to eventually get every house in here on solar power."

"You just be careful with Jacob and Channelside. Those people aren't worth dying for. Brad and Eric are cool guys but the people of Channelside don't care about you and us. They only care about themselves," says Matt.

"You are right Matt, but I have to try to help them with Jacob. At least find out what Jacob is up to with Channelside."

Bobby G, Matt, Phil, and I unload the tons of awesome stuff we got from Davis Island.

"How much you think this pasta maker costs?" asks Phil.

"I don't know. Those things can be a pretty penny," says Bobby G.

Phil and Matt take some stuff into Matt's house.

Bobby G and I walk over to Shaun's house.

Jon and Shaun are finishing up unloading their vehicles.

Jon is charging his electric car in Shaun's garage.

"I'm glad you are going to talk with Jacob about Channelside," says Jon.

"I know you are Jon. I know you want me to work things out with Jacob and Channelside."

"You are going to talk with Jacob, right?" asks Jon.

"Yeah. I wasn't lying to Brad and Eric. I'm a man of my word. You should know that about me, Jon."

Jon says, "I know. Just wanted to make sure. I know you are a man of integrity and trust."

Shaun asks, "Did you see some of the things those rich people had in their homes? Some of those homes were tacky as hell."

"Having money doesn't mean having good taste," says Bobby G.

"Those homes were pretty sweet though. DJ's house was pretty awesome. Everything was marble. I can't wait to see the homes on Bayshore Boulevard."

"Why? What's Bayshore Boulevard?" asks Shaun.

"Bayshore Boulevard is a road that is right on the bay. Each home is a couple million dollars easily. Bayshore is where they have Gasparilla. I took you guys there one year."

"Oh yeah. Gasparilla was fun. Tons of beads, beer, and boobs," says Shaun.

We finish unloading the vehicles and go into our homes.

Jon drives his new electric car to his home.

Phil drives his SUV into the driveway of his house.

Shaun connects his electric truck to the vehicle charger in his garage.

Matt and Kylie sit on the sofa.

Matt puts his hand on Kylie's stomach.

Kylie and Matt both smile at each other.

I walk into my house.

Milo greets me and rubs against my left leg.

Callie is drinking water from her bowl in the kitchen.

Lauren is singing in our master bathroom.

I take off my shoes and place them on the mat next to my front door.

I lock my front door.

I bend down and pet Milo on his head.

I walk into the kitchen and see Callie drinking water from her bowl.

Callie meows at me.

"Hey Ya-Ya," I say to Callie.

I open my refrigerator and grab a flavored electrolyte beverage.

I drink the entire 32-ounce bottle.

I'm dehydrated from working outside on Davis Island and unloading the vehicles.

I walk into my master bedroom.

Lauren hears me come in and stops singing.

"Hey honey," says Lauren as she pokes her head out of the master bathroom.

"You almost done in there? I want to take a shower," I say to Lauren as I take off my shirt.

"Take it off!" shouts Lauren.

I smile at Lauren's comment.

Lauren says, "I'll be right out."

Lauren finishes up in the bathroom and walks over to me.

"How did it go? Did you miss me and my bow skills?" asks Lauren.

"It went well. I always miss the skills of my wife when we go out."

Lauren asks, "Get anything good?"

"Yeah actually. We got four electric vehicles. Tons of supplies and stuff from the homes on Davis Island and we got fish from Brad."

"Fish! Yuck! I need some chicken," says Lauren.

"I'm still working on the chicken, but you'll have to try some fish. We need more protein in our diet."

"I'll try some, but I think we get some good protein from the food we have around here," says Lauren.

I kiss Lauren and go into the bathroom.

I turn on the shower and let it warm up.

I look in the mirror at my beard and long hair.

"I'll need you to cut my hair later! I look pretty terrible right now!"

Lauren replies, "I can do it after your shower, if you want!"

"Sounds good!"

I grab my electric razor and trim my beard. I haven't shaved in several weeks, and my beard has started to get overgrown and itchy.

I finish up shaving and jump in the shower.

As I'm showering, I think about the recent days and what we have been able to accomplish. I'm happy that everyone is safe, and our neighborhood is doing well.

I'm usually an optimistic person with a strong sense of reality.

Life isn't always good and bad. Life is all about ups and downs, peaks and valleys, highs and lows.

I feel that we are in a high right now, and it probably won't last. I just hope that the low point doesn't cancel out the highs that we are currently having.

A satellite phone rings.

RING! RING!

"Sir, you have a call from General Godfrey," says Rebecca to Rich through the phone intercom.

"Thank you, Rebecca," says Rich.

Rich takes a deep breath and picks up the phone.

Rich hits the line one button on the phone and asks,

"General Godfrey, what can I help you with?"

General Godfrey says, "Captain Bailey, I have some new orders for you. We will be sending you several new groups and teams of military personnel."

"What are the new orders?" asks Rich.

"We are starting a new project. The first of its kind," says General Godfrey.

"Great. What is the project? What are the details?" asks Rich.

General Godfrey replies, "It's project Weaponize. I will have a large C130 come to MacDill with the staff needed to implement the new orders and start the project."

"What is project Weaponize?" asks Rich.

"All the details will be explained when my people get there," says General Godfrey.

"When will they be leaving for MacDill?" asks Rich.

"They already left. They should be coming your way shortly," says General Godfrey.

"Yes sir. Thank you, sir. I won't let you down," says Rich.

General Godfrey says, "I hope not Captain. The world is counting on this new project. The world is falling apart. We have suffered heavy losses in the U.S., and overseas."

Rich replies, "I'm sorry to hear that. We are losing the battle against the dead?"

"We are losing, but it's not over yet. We have some plans in motion and it starts with the project coming your way. Project Weaponize is a new order. It was just developed by our scientists and doctors in D.C.," says General Godfrey.

"Will we be seeing you soon General?" asks Rich.

"No, not anytime soon, but I will eventually make my way to Tampa Bay with my team," says General Godfrey.

"I look forward to the new project and the new orders. Thank you for choosing MacDill for the project," says Rich.

"Didn't have any choice. We don't have many military bases still standing on the East coast. We have some in Texas and on the West Coast, but MacDill is the best option we have on the East Coast of the U.S.," says General Godfrey.

"Well, again General, I won't let you down. Whatever your group needs for the project, they will have," says Rich.

General Godfrey replies, "Thank you, Captain. I will be in touch with you over the next couple of days. Good luck with project Weaponize. You are going to need it."

TO BE CONTINUED...